Gift-Wrapped Family

Lois Richer

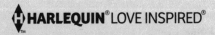

LOVE INSPIRED BOOKS

PLEASE RECYCLE · THIS PRODUCT IS RECYCLABLE

Recycling programs for this product may not exist in your area.

ISBN-13: 978-0-373-81878-5

Gift-Wrapped Family

www.Harlequin.com

Printed in U.S.A.

"You said Lily is five?" Mia hiccuped a sob.

"That means my late husband and his secretary were together about as long as we were married. Why stay married to me if he was in love with someone else?" She dashed a tear from her cheek. "Why not marry her? Create a family with her?"

"There's no way we'll ever know." Caleb refused to restate the obvious lure of Mia's money. He wasn't sure she knew how much her mother had left her, but his sources told him the number was high, very high.

"He said he never wanted to have children."

"Judging by the amount of attention he paid Lily, I'm guessing that part was true."

"I wish I could have a child." She began to weep as though her heart was broken.

Caleb watched helplessly, thinking what a wonderful mother this caring woman would make. Somehow he knew that Mia was cut from the same cloth as his mother had been. Mia would welcome a child, make him or her feel loved, the most important person in her world. Mia would intrinsically know how and when to give a hug.

Things Caleb lacked. Because of his father.

Lois Richer loves traveling, swimming and quilting, but mostly she loves writing stories that show God's boundless love for His precious children. As she says, "His love never changes or gives up. It's always waiting for me. My stories feature imperfect characters learning that love doesn't mean attaining perfection. Love is about keeping on keeping on." You can contact Lois via email, loisricher@yahoo.com, or on Facebook (LoisRicherAuthor).

Books by Lois Richer

Love Inspired

Family Ties

A Dad for Her Twins
Rancher Daddy
Gift-Wrapped Family

Northern Lights

North Country Hero
North Country Family
North Country Mom
North Country Dad

Healing Hearts

A Doctor's Vow
Yuletide Proposal
Perfectly Matched

Love for All Seasons

The Holiday Nanny
A Baby by Easter
A Family for Summer

Visit the Author Profile page at Harlequin.com for more titles.

You shall love the Lord your God
with all your heart, with all your soul,
and with all your strength.

—Deuteronomy 6:5

Chapter One

"This can't be the place."

Lawyer Caleb Grant matched the address on the paper in his hand with the crooked numbers on a small bungalow that had seen better days in this Canadian neighborhood of Calgary, Alberta, and grimaced.

"Are you sure you gave me the correct address?" he asked into his phone. Having confirmed his location, he opened the rickety gate.

The serious disrepair of the house contrasted with the garden in front, which bloomed in a riot of color. Mia Granger must be a dab hand with plants. How could a woman with this tender gift for gardening ignore his plea to help a bereaved child?

Before Caleb could reach the end of the cobbled path, the weathered front door opened. A slim woman with masses of strawberry blonde hair tumbling around her shoulders stepped outside and reached for the mailbox. Her hand stilled when she saw him.

"C-can I help you?" she asked in a voice so quiet he barely heard it.

"I'm looking for Mia Granger. Does she live here?" Caleb watched her ivory skin pale.

"I'm Mia. Are you another bill collector?" she said in a breathless voice. "I'm sorry but—"

"I'm a lawyer with Family Ties. It's an adoption agency in Buffalo Gap." He saw no recognition on her face. "Someone called you about me."

"No one called," she murmured in a scared voice, golden-red hair shivering in the wash of sunlight sneaking through a few dappled leaves left on a towering poplar tree.

"They should have." Caleb frowned. Mayor Marsha had talked him into coming here. She'd also promised she'd notify widow Granger of his arrival. When a flicker of worry widened Mia's emerald eyes, he decided he could deal with Marsha later. "I'm here about Lily."

"Who?" As hard as Caleb searched her puzzled face, he saw no sign that she was prevaricating. "I think you must have the wrong—"

"She's the five-year-old daughter of your husband, Harlan Granger, and his mistress, Reba Jones." Though Caleb hated to be so blunt, there was no easy way to do this. "Lily lost both her parents in the car accident that took your husband two weeks ago."

"How dare you?" Mia Granger gasped. One hand grabbed onto the shaky wrought iron railing.

"Are you all right?" Troubled by her ashen face, Caleb reached out to steady her, but the woman backed away.

"You've got everything wrong," she insisted in a tearful voice. "Reba was Harlan's *secretary*. They certainly didn't have a child together. Please leave." She turned away.

"I'm so sorry to trouble you." Caleb's instincts told him he couldn't leave now. He had to reach this woman's heart, for Lily's sake.

"Then, don't." Her pale, pinched face implored him to leave her alone. But Caleb couldn't do that.

"I've checked the birth records," he said softly. "Lily *is* their child."

Mia paled even more. She shook her head.

"It's true. Please, may I please come inside and talk to you?"

Her distrust of him showed in the gold sparks that changed her emerald eyes to hazel. Given the deceitful husband she'd married, Caleb didn't blame her for that. But he was also curious. Torn between trying to believe she was truly bewildered but feeling suspicious that she was trying to avoid him as she had his phone calls, Caleb pressed harder.

"I truly do not want to add to your pain." He employed the calming tone he often used with a skittery witness on the stand. "I only want to help this little girl." He pulled a picture from his chest pocket and held it out. "Lily Jones."

Mia looked at the photo. When her eyes widened and her trembling lips parted in a gasp, Caleb knew he was making up lost ground. But then he saw something puzzling in her gaze—yearning?

"She's a beautiful child, isn't she?" Caleb hated causing this gentle woman more grief, but he was determined she understand that Lily's future was at stake.

"The eyes—they're quite startling." Mia's gaze remained riveted on the picture.

"The same color as Harlan Granger's."

"Many people have dark blue eyes." Mia finally handed him the photo with a sigh. "I suppose you'd better come in," she said in obvious resignation. She allowed him through and then closed the door. "This way."

Caleb followed, noting that the interior of the house had probably once been magnificent. Though it hadn't aged gracefully, it was spotless. The Victorian-style sofa Mia indicated with the wave of one hand was as desperately uncomfortable as it looked, but Caleb sat on it anyway, keeping his face impassive.

Mia Granger stood in front of the massive bay window in a puddle of bright October sunshine. She wore a pair of shabby jeans that looked too big and a faded teal sweater that drooped from her lean curves. Her beautiful hair flowed over her shoulders like a pale copper cape. When she caught Caleb staring, she crossed her thin arms across her chest defensively.

Caleb couldn't stop staring. Backlit by the sun, the shape of Mia's face brought memories of his mother, the mother he'd loved so dearly and lost to his murderous father.

"What was your name?" she prodded.

"Caleb Grant. As I said, I represent an adoption agency called Family Ties." Caleb shook off his memories and concentrated on the delicate woman in front of him. *Do your job*, his brain ordered.

"Lily is one of their children waiting to be adopted?" Mia sank onto an armchair that could have sat three of her and nestled against the folds of a colorful quilt draped across the back of it.

"Not exactly. I wanted to explain when I called, but your phone is always busy or no one answers." He studied her face, surprised by the flush of red in her cheeks.

"Sometimes I take it off the hook. Or I don't answer. I can't take any more calls from those to whom we owe money." Mia stared at her hands.

Owe money? Caleb hadn't expected that. It threw him off, made him wonder if she was trying to con him. He decided to turn the conversation back to Lily because Mia had made a connection with her picture.

"Lily may eventually be adopted. First we have to sort out her custody and what she's owed from her father's estate." Caleb decided that while Mia might look innocent, she wasn't stupid. She immediately straightened.

"Mr. Grant," she began in a regal tone.

"Caleb," he interrupted.

"Caleb," she agreed softly. "You think my late husband is this child's father. I assure you you're wrong." She continued, her voice growing steadily stronger. "I don't have any money to give Lily. If I did, I would certainly help the poor child." She paused for a moment, then murmured, "I never knew Reba had a daughter, but then I didn't know Harlan's staff well."

"Lily was *his* child, too," Caleb insisted. A new stain of red flushed her cheeks, bringing his sympathy. If he'd known Mia was unaware of her husband's affair, he'd have handled this differently.

"I sympathize with Lily because as a child I lost my mother suddenly, too," she said, ignoring his remark. "But I'm sorry, there's nothing I can do for her. I owe money myself." The receding blush returned and deepened. She lowered her gaze.

"But, Mia, your husband's estate must be considerable." Caleb couldn't believe her temerity. He knew from his research that Granger was loaded. He'd dealt with many prevaricators in his career and was oddly disappointed to realize sweet-looking Mia was one of them. But that sweetness wouldn't stop him from seeking Lily's rightful inheritance.

"Why do you assume that?" Mia's gaze made him feel guilty for poking into her private world. "My husband was a lawyer, but we're certainly not wealthy. You can see how we live." She glared at him. "Harlan had to take whatever cases he was offered. In fact, he often had to go out of town to find work."

The certainty in Mia Granger's voice bothered Caleb. She looked and sounded as though she genuinely believed what she was saying. But if they were so hard up, why hadn't her husband moved his office from its expensive downtown location to a less pricey area?

"What about the ranch? There's a lot of land attached to that, valuable land." He studied her intently, surprised when her forehead furrowed.

"What ranch? Harlan and I were married for six years. We never owned a ranch." Caleb figured she saw something in his face, because the last of her words faltered before she whispered, "Have we?"

"What has your lawyer told you?" Caleb figured his best hope was to untie this mess without further alienating her.

"You mean Trent Vilang? Harlan's partner," she explained, as if Caleb didn't already know that. "I've been feeling unwell since Harlan's death, so Trent's only told me the bare bones about the estate."

"And that is?" For Lily's sake, Caleb pressed, ignoring her frown at his inquisitiveness.

"Trent said there was barely enough money to pay off the firm's bills and Harlan's cre—" Mia gulped. The sheen of tears washed her eyes, but she lifted her chin and finished with quiet dignity, "His cremation."

"I see." As Caleb's uncertainty mushroomed he glanced around, searching for a clue to his next step. His glance stalled on the oil painting over the fireplace. "Lovely painting. Who is it?" he asked, as if he didn't know.

"My mother."

"Your mother was Pia Standish?" He was speaking to the daughter of the woman he'd admired most of his life? Now nothing made sense.

"Did you know her?" Mia's curiosity was evident.

"I did." Caleb declined to discuss his childhood interaction with the legendary legal genius, but he couldn't suppress a smile remembering Pia's potent courtroom condemnation of his father. "I was her client once. I never forgot her."

"I never saw her at work, but I've heard she was a good lawyer." There was something wistful in Mia's voice.

"Pia was beyond merely good," Caleb told her. "Her firm, Standish Law, was the biggest in the province. I remember seeing well-known people in her office."

"I used to think we were well off," Mia mused reflectively. "At first I thought that's why Harlan agreed to marry me."

"Excuse me?" Caleb stared at her. Who would need to be coerced to marry this lovely woman?

"I was seventeen and in boarding school when I was summoned home. My mother told me she'd been diagnosed with brain cancer. She told me that for my own protection I was to marry this lawyer who worked for her, Harlan Granger." Mia's voice faltered. "She said he'd take care of me."

"He was much older. Why would he agree?" Caleb asked.

"Money, I suppose. Harlan received my mother's law firm as a kind of dowry." Her green eyes grew troubled. "Mother had a nice house."

"I was there once." Caleb remembered his awe at visiting the huge mansion.

"Harlan sold it after she died," Mia said, staring at something Caleb couldn't see. "I thought it should have brought us plenty of money, but Harlan said Mother had run up large debts trying to find a cure. He sold the house to pay off what she owed." Her lips pinched together. "I was sorry to lose some of our things," she added in a small, hurt voice.

Mia's defenselessness, her sadness touched Caleb. He gave her time to regroup while he shot off a text message to his paralegal. Find out everything about Mia Standish Granger. Stat.

"That's why your claim is so incredible." Mia rose. "I've lived here since I married Harlan. We've had to be very frugal while he revived her firm. We— I'm not rich, Mr. Grant."

"Your mother didn't leave you any money of your own?" He searched her face, no longer certain she was lying.

"I'm afraid not. Everything goes to pay the bills." A tiny smile flitted across her incredibly beautiful face. "Would you like some tea?"

"I would. Thank you." Caleb hated tea, especially herbal tea, but he'd learned the fine art of pretending to drink it when his best friend Lara was alive, because she'd loved tea and he'd wanted to love her. It still rankled that he'd never felt the strong emotion for her that Lara claimed to feel for him, to realize that he couldn't love anyone because of what his father had done.

Caleb shoved those uncomfortable thoughts away and concentrated on Mia. She had to be pretending her marriage was solid, but he was determined she'd admit the truth before he left here, and if that required tea drinking, that was what he'd do.

"Let's go to the kitchen. It's warmer there." Mia waited for his nod, then led the way. "Have a seat," she invited as she pulled out a mismatched chair from the big oak table. "Do you have a particularly favorite tea? I have a good variety."

Caleb blinked when she opened a cupboard door to reveal neatly organized rows of small packages of tea. "Do you ever!"

"My stomach's been upset since Harlan—died." Mia regained her composure. "Trent's been a dear friend. He consulted an herbalist for me and brings home teas for me to try. They haven't helped yet, but..." She shrugged and smiled. "Take your time deciding which you'd like."

"Any kind is fine." A previous investigation on Trent Vilang had left Caleb with tons of questions. "Dear Trent" had befriended widows before and some of those ladies had become very ill. Caleb kept his reservations about the man to himself as Mia moved around her broken-down kitchen.

Anything that could sparkle in this room did, but the house and especially this kitchen needed to be gutted, and no amount of soap or elbow grease could fix that. Then suddenly, beyond the kitchen, he spied bright sunshine.

"Would you rather sit in the sunroom?" Mia asked, noting his interest. "It's quite warm today because the sun's out. That's when I love working there the most."

"What is your work?" Caleb's curiosity built. Her job was one detail he hadn't yet discovered. Mia looked too delicate for any kind of physical work. Cellist. Or maybe pianist, he guessed.

"Oh, it's nothing," she demurred.

Caleb thought that sounded like someone else's assessment. But he said nothing as she rinsed out a small brown china teapot.

"I dream up designs for quilt fabrics," Mia finally said almost apologetically.

"Oh." That fit, Caleb decided, then realized that though he'd just met Mia, he'd instinctively known that employment suited her. *Getting too involved. Maintain your distance,* his brain scolded. That was difficult to do with this intriguing woman.

"When my designs are incorporated into fabric, the company sends me a bolt of each. I then make up several quilts to feature various aspects of the fabric and how to use it. It's nothing like the law," she apologized. "Nothing at all like the important work Harlan did."

"Why should it be like his?" Caleb wished he'd met the man who'd made his wife feel that her work was trivial. "It's just as important to have beautiful things in the world as it is to have the law." She had the tray ready. "Can I carry something?"

"The tea?" Mia smiled her thanks and led the way into a sunroom that took his breath away. Vibrantly painted canvases lay sprawled around the room, flowers in riotous color, a seaside scene, the cool white on white of deepest winter. "I'm sorry it's so crowded. Harlan was always after me to stack these away." Mia gulped, then reached to move one.

"Please leave it. They're beautiful," Caleb said, and meant it.

"Oh." Startled green eyes met his before quickly veering away. "Thank you. Please sit wherever you like." She poured their tea and then sat across from him on a rickety wicker chair whose quilted cushion said it had been well loved. "Mr. Grant—"

"Call me Caleb." Nothing in her expression to suggest she was flirting or playing games, but Caleb clung to his defenses anyway. He had a job to do. He couldn't let her sad situation get to him.

"Very well, Caleb. Well, other than serving you tea, I don't know how I can help you." Mia Granger frowned. He thought it a shame to mar the beauty of her face, but the helplessness in her next words irritated him. "What is it you expect of me?"

"I'm not sure." Caleb remembered Lily's parting words. *Can you find me a home, Uncle Caleb? Please?* That plea from Lara's niece broke his heart. "I came here hoping to learn the truth, but I'm not sure you know it."

"Whose truth? Yours?" Mia sipped her tea. "Like your claim that Harlan had a ranch."

"He did. Riverbend Ranch." Caleb thought her eyes widened for a second.

"We didn't have a ranch. If we had, why would

we live here?" she asked with some asperity. "Why would Harlan need to travel for his business?"

"Are you sure he did 'need' to?" Though she tried to hide it, Caleb had seen Mia's reaction to the word *Riverbend.* Now his senses were on high alert. She was hiding something, and he intended to find out what, despite that gaze of wide-eyed innocence.

In Caleb's experience very few women could carry off a claim of innocence. Lara had been one, but he wasn't totally certain about Mia because there were even fewer women who managed to tug at his compassion, and she did.

Surprised by the emotions she raised in him, Caleb decided he'd best be on guard around Mia Granger. Anything but friendship was impossible.

Caleb Grant was the most handsome man Mia had ever met. Tall, lean and dark, he exuded confidence, something she'd always admired but lacked. At the moment, Mia didn't like the way he studied her with his silver-cold eyes. Nor did she like how his tall muscular body invaded the place where she'd mostly lived alone. She especially didn't like the calculation in his voice, as if he expected to catch her in a lie.

Caleb's suggestion that Harlan had been unfaithful stung. The situation hadn't been ideal, but she'd done her best to be a good wife after a simple ceremony at city hall had joined them in holy matrimony. No, they didn't share a strong, fairy-tale love. But he'd kept her safe after her mother died and she was grateful. Mia mourned his death. Now she was all alone.

But even though they hadn't *really* been married, not the way other couples were, that didn't mean Harlan would have done what Caleb Grant said.

On the tail of those thoughts, snippets of details dawned. Hadn't she always felt uneasy over Harlan's frequent late-night meetings with Reba? And the way Reba touched his shoulder so fondly before jerking her hand away when she realized Mia had come to the office for her one and only visit? That had stuck in Mia's mind for ages, especially after Harlan had ordered her to stay away. But that didn't mean…

She shoved her wayward thoughts out of her mind. She'd think about Harlan and Reba later. Right now Caleb Grant was here. He was a lawyer. Maybe he'd have some advice that could help sort out her pressing financial problems. Inhaling a breath of courage, she dived in.

"Caleb, this land, er, ranch you speak of Harlan owning. Where is it?"

"Riverbend Ranch is outside Buffalo Gap, about thirty-five miles from here." Caleb's innocent gaze turned cunning. "Do you know of it?"

He'd seen her reaction to that name, so there was no point in pretending. Mia rose, walked to her big battered desk and removed a thin file. She held it out.

"What's this?" he asked, taking it from her.

"It's about Harlan's estate, according to Trent, Harlan's partner and also my lawyer." She sat down, lifted her cup and took a refreshing drink. "Go ahead and look. Riverbend is a lawsuit my husband was handling, if I understand those papers correctly."

His eyes searched hers. Mia held it until—there went her stomach again, clenching and whirling as if some flu bug had hold of it. A minute earlier she'd felt perfectly fine, but now she closed her eyes and waited for her stomach to settle.

"Are you all right?" Caleb's eyes bored into hers.

"A little flu. I hope you don't catch it." Mia sat perfectly still, hands in her lap. When he didn't move she said, "Please read it. I'll wait."

She watched him, amazed by the speed with which he scanned the documents she'd taken hours to peruse. Less than two minutes later he looked up, his mouth stretched tight in a grim line.

"You see? There's nothing about a ranch or money," she said, her voice dropping at the stern look on his face. "I'm not lying."

"This is all Trent gave you? Nothing more?"

Mia shook her head.

"Did you sign anything recently?" Caleb voice was tight and sharp.

"Of course. There were a number of papers Trent needed me to sign to deal with my husband's estate." She shivered, intensely disliking this inquisition but not sure how to stop it.

Caleb had said he was a lawyer and she was sure he was a good one, though she'd never heard of this adoption agency, Family Ties. But as a lawyer he would know how to get people to say things—she should be on guard. He might actually be from some collection company.

"Do you have copies of what you signed?" Caleb demanded.

"No. Trent said he'd copy them at the office and bring them back. He hasn't yet returned with them." Something in the frost of his silver-steel eyes made her shiver. "Is—is anything wrong?" she asked hesitantly, and reared back when he nodded.

"Yes. I think quite a lot is wrong." Caleb closed his eyes and rubbed his temples. "Mia, this will be hard to hear, but you must listen because it's the truth. I've been investigating your husband's affairs, for Lily's sake. Nothing I've found indicates he was hard up for money or that he or Trent had taken on a new client in months."

"But that can't be." She struggled to sort it out and looked at him. She saw nothing but honesty in his expression. Could it be true? "Then, what were he and Reba doing on all these trips?"

"That's what we need to discover." Caleb

glanced at his ringing phone, read the message and frowned. When he lifted his gaze to hers, the icy anger made her shiver. "Did you know your lawyer filed documents this morning seeking to take over all your affairs because he says you are incompetent?"

"What?" Mia couldn't believe Trent would do such a thing.

"We need to act fast to protect you. Call Trent," Caleb ordered. "Ask him to come here. Beg if that will get him here immediately."

"Why?" She was afraid to trust Caleb, to trust anyone, yet there was something in Caleb's hard, cold eyes that reassured her he would not be part of any wrongdoing.

She didn't truly trust him, but if he was right about Trent, who else could she turn to for help? She picked up the phone and pressed in her lawyer's number.

"Trent, it's Mia. Can you c-come here? P-please? It's urgent." She listened to his gruff excuses but said nothing. Finally he agreed. "Th-thank you." She hung up.

"Well?" Caleb Grant's silver eyes probed hers.

"H-he'll be here in half an hour. But I have no idea what I'll say to him. What do I do?" Even asking the question scared Mia.

"I'll speak for you." Caleb's fierce glare faded slightly. "I know it hurts and you don't want to think about it right now, but Harlan Granger was not the man you thought he was and neither is his partner. Something's been going on, something more than an affair. I intend to find out what. Okay?"

A picture of Harlan and Reba together, laughing and loving, sharing a child, while she sat alone, would not leave Mia's mind. Her husband had always been cool, distant and businesslike. He'd promised her mother he'd care for her. Surely he couldn't, wouldn't have turned to another... Suddenly her stomach heaved and Mia could think of nothing but escape.

"Excuse me." She hurried to the bathroom, where she was violently sick.

Oh, Lord, I feel so bad. And something is terribly wrong. Please help me.

She'd barely had a chance to regain her breath when *he* rapped on the door.

"I'm all right," she called, irritated by her weak voice. "I'll be out in a minute."

"We need to hurry." Caleb's voice left little room for argument. In fact, he was leaning against the hall table impatiently tapping his foot when she emerged. Feeling disheveled and weaker than she'd ever been, Mia walked slowly to the sunroom and sat down. She reached out to take her cup, but Caleb ordered, "Don't touch that."

Mia flinched and drew her hand away. "Why?"

"I believe there's something in your tea that makes you sick." His tone was harsh.

"Caleb, that's ridiculous," she burst out. Maybe he was wrong about Harlan… "Trent would never—"

"I'm pretty sure he's done it before," he said, certainty in his voice. "You've been drinking the stuff for days and you've felt ill about that long, right?"

"Yes. But—" Mia stared at her cup as frightening scenarios played through her mind.

"That tea should be tested. The police will be here shortly." Caleb's lips tightened. "They can do that. I've also ordered an ambulance."

She felt herself sway and grabbed the table. "Why?"

"To check you out and take blood samples that will discern if something's off in your system." Caleb leaned forward and covered her hand with his. His touch sent ripples of awareness up her arm. "Mia, you won't like what I'm about to say."

"Is it worse than you saying Harlan was having an affair? That he had—a child with his secretary?" She had to force the words out. When Caleb nodded she saw pity on his face. She did not want his pity, so she straightened her spine. "Go ahead, say it."

"I believe that Harlan, along with Trent, was running some kind of scheme to secrete money. After Harlan died in the car accident, I believe Trent saw a way to get that money for himself." Caleb frowned. "I think Riverbend Ranch is the reason, though I haven't yet made all the connections. In order to get the ranch, Trent needs you out of the way."

Mia sat in stupefied silence as Caleb explained about the ranch her husband had supposedly bought. He spoke of a petition for divorce Harlan had supposedly filed the day he died and listed a money trail Caleb claimed he was still uncovering.

Dazed and ill, horrified to imagine the man she'd married was capable of such betrayal, Mia tuned out the pain and hurt that threatened to overwhelm her. How could it be possible? How could God have betrayed her trust? She'd believed for so long that He was there, protecting her, comforting her in her lonely marriage. Now it felt as though He'd played a horrible trick, just as Caleb claimed Harlan and Trent had. It was too much to deal with.

Her brain numb, she sat silent as Caleb told the same story to the police when they arrived. They waited in the kitchen when she let Trent inside. Mia could see guilt build in Trent's eyes as Caleb pummeled him with questions. She couldn't bear to believe that this friend, one of the few she had and the only one she'd truly trusted since Harlan's death, had deliberately set out to hurt her.

While Trent scrambled for a defense, Mia held her whirling emotions at bay. For now she'd be strong. But in her heart of hearts she knew she believed Caleb's accusations. So deep was her feeling of betrayal, she couldn't even manage a silent plea to God for help. He'd let this happen. How could she trust Him again?

A detective arrived, showed Trent a warrant for his arrest and after a few questions told the officers to take her lawyer to the station. The detective seemed to know Caleb and the two whispered together before Caleb introduced her to Detective Ed Gray.

"Our police station has been investigating Harlan Granger for several months via a request from the IRS who are tracking what they believe is unreported income," the detective told Mia. "This new information about your lawyer adds to our investigation. For that reason I hope you'll allow these paramedics to take a sample of your blood. Then I'll need to ask you some questions."

"Okay." Mia remained silent when he beckoned the paramedics forward. They took several vials of blood, which were then handed to an officer, who sealed them in an evidence bag and left with another officer.

"They'll have our lab run tests on your blood," the detective explained. "As a precaution, I'd like the paramedics to check you over now."

Mia nodded and the two medical people got to work.

"Your vitals seem to be getting stronger," they told her sometime later. "You'll be okay." The detective thanked and dismissed them.

Mia was rolling down her sleeve when two men came out of her kitchen carrying evidence bags that contained her teas. Her heart sank a little further. Could it be true—had Trent been trying to poison her?

"Now for the questions." Detective Ed Gray's face tightened.

Mia did her best to answer everything he asked, even though some of his questions puzzled her. From time to time she glanced at Caleb. His gaze never wavered from her. But it was not a flattering look. It was a suspicious look that asked how she could have been so naive.

In retrospect Mia asked herself the same thing as she finally accepted that she'd been incredibly stupid to have trusted her husband. But it had never occurred to her to not trust him because her mother had. In fact, she'd placed Mia's life in his hands. And Trent was Harlan's trusted partner. So why— She silently groaned, tired of trying to make sense of it.

As the weight of her situation settled on her shoulders, Mia wanted to be left alone. And yet she didn't want to be alone to think about Harlan's betrayal. They hadn't had a normal marriage, but to imagine that he'd betray her with Reba—

One word played over and over in her mind. *Betrayed.* And following it—*you can't trust anyone.*

"Mrs. Granger?" The detective touched her shoulder.

"Sorry. What did you say?" She forced herself to concentrate.

"I know all of this must come as a shock, especially right after your husband's death, but one of my officers has phoned to say Trent just admitted to lacing your teas with a substance to make you sick." He gave her a sympathetic smile. "Our medical people advise drinking plenty of fluids to flush it out of your system. You can thank Caleb for acting on his instincts. There should be no long-lasting effects."

"Thank you." Mia looked at the lawyer and the detective, not knowing what else to say. Everything seemed surreal, like being an actor in some horrible play she couldn't escape.

"The total of what Trent and your husband perpetrated isn't yet clear, but we've launched a full investigation," the detective explained.

"Oh." If possible, Mia now felt worse. The rest? There was more betrayal in store for her?

"I suggest you retain new legal counsel who can begin sorting through your husband's affairs." The detective inclined his head toward Caleb. "I can vouch for Caleb. He'll be straightforward with you. And to be frank, I think you're going to need his help."

Relief swamped her. Surely if the detective trusted Caleb, she could, too, if only for a little while, just until things were straightened out. A niggle of hope flickered to life. Maybe with

Caleb's help she could finally dare to imagine a future with hope. *Please, Lord?*

"Any questions?" the detective asked.

"Why did Trent want to hurt me?" Mia asked.

"I can't answer that yet." He gave Caleb a sideways glance. "But I will find out, I promise you."

"Thank you," she said again. A thought pricked her brain. "I don't know if it's important, but Trent didn't buy all of those teas. Harlan brought some home from several of his trips. So if Trent did try to hurt me, and I'm still struggling with that, only some of the tea would be affected."

The two men shared a look before the detective nodded, then said goodbye.

"What do I do now?" she asked Caleb, feeling lost, when the detective was gone.

"Were all your bank accounts joint?" When she nodded he said, "Let's go."

"Where?" His hand on her arm urged her to move. Mia grabbed her handbag from the hall table and followed Caleb outside. She jerked her arm free of his grip to lock the door. "Where are we going?"

"To a bank so you can open an account in your own name." He held open the door of a luxurious black car. "A bank where you haven't dealt before. You'll withdraw everything from your old accounts and put it in there."

"Why?" Confused and upset with questions tumbling through her brain, not the least of which had to do with Harlan and a dark blue–eyed little girl named Lily, Mia protested, but Caleb was adamant.

"If my suspicions are right, what you signed were papers giving Trent legal custody of your affairs, which will allow him to drain every resource you have as dry as a stone." He shook his head when she would have protested. "If he is released today, he could make the transactions immediately and you'll be broke until everything's sorted, which could be a very long time."

"I'm broke now," she whispered.

"That's according to Trent, who isn't the best source for the truth." Caleb pulled to a stop in front of a small bank, turned and asked in a harsh tone, "Don't you get it?"

"I get that you believe Trent was stealing from me," she whispered, afraid to believe it but more afraid to disbelieve this man. "I don't get why."

"Greed." Caleb Grant's face softened as he looked at her. Transfixed by the change of his gorgeous eyes from ice to melted silver, Mia barely flinched when his hand lifted to brush the swath of curls off her face. "It was greed, Mia."

"For money that you think Harlan had." She sighed. "Which he didn't. I don't understand."

"I have a hunch greed is something a woman like you could never understand." For a moment Caleb's compassion almost undid Mia. Until his mouth firmed and the frost returned to his eyes. "Here's the bank. Better get the transfer started."

Despite her reservations, Mia had to depend on him; she had no one else. But she had to be careful. Though she knew little about men, she knew that despite the help he'd given her, Caleb Grant didn't suffer naive women like her easily.

It would take a lot for Mia to trust again.

Chapter Two

"I can't be your legal adviser, Mia. I represent Family Ties. Our intent is to seek reparation from your husband's estate for his daughter, Lily Jones." Caleb swallowed. "I have a conflict of interest."

Wasn't that the truth? Caleb had been all gung ho to oppose Mia when he left his office this morning. Somehow in meeting her, hearing her side of the story and seeing how ill Trent had made her, he'd done an about-face. He now wanted to help Mia, but his own legal position combined with the loss and confusion filling her lovely face during their elevator ride to the twelfth floor made him feel utterly powerless.

"What are we doing here?" Mia asked.

"I have a very good friend, a lawyer, who is one of the best. That's who we're going to see. She's straight as an arrow. You can trust her and I promise she'll help you." Caleb wished he could be the one to guide Mia through the difficult parts to come and reassure her each step of the way, though he wasn't clear on why it suddenly seemed imperative for him to protect her. Maybe it was because he hated seeing the innocent conned and Mia was certainly innocent. He now had no doubt about that.

Bella Jourdain was the best in her field. If anyone could get Mia out of the mess her husband and his partner had made, Bella could. Once they were shown into her inner sanctum, he hugged the older woman heartily then leaned back to study her lined face.

"How come you never get older, Bella?" Caleb asked.

"Clean living, kiddo." Her almost black eyes scanned Mia. "This is Pia's daughter?"

Caleb introduced them. Then he laid out the problem for Bella, having received a text confirmation that his office had already faxed her most of the pertinent information on the case so she wouldn't be completely in the dark.

"You believe the partner, Trent, has been embezzling?" Bella mused, scribbling madly.

"I suspect Harlan Granger was doing the same." Caleb wished he could spare Mia when she frowned at him as if he'd betrayed her. He continued because it was the only path he knew to get Mia and Lily justice. "My assistant just dug up old court records indicating that Mia's mother, Pia Standish, left an in-trust account for her daughter to be administered by Granger until Mia was twenty-one."

"But I'm twenty-three and I've never heard of any account," Mia protested.

"Exactly." Caleb glanced at Bella, one eyebrow arched.

The older woman tapped a pencil against her lips for several seconds, then rose. "You'll have to leave now, Caleb."

"But I haven't finished." He glared at his old friend.

"You've finished here. You represent Family Ties and Granger's child. We both know you can't be privy to any further personal conferencing between me and my client. I appreciate your help, but I must protect my client and you. So it's time for you to leave." Bella walked to the door and pulled it open. "Sorry."

Knowing she was right but frustrated that he hadn't yet found the answers he sought for Lily, Caleb walked to the door.

"But he's been helping me. I want Caleb to stay," Mia said.

"Bella is your lawyer, Mia, and she's very good at what she does. Her concern is your interest, and until she's got things sorted out, you must listen to what she says," Caleb reassured her. Funny how quickly he'd come to like Mia, how fast he'd moved from resenting her for Lily's sake to trying to help her. "I'll wait outside."

"Okay." Mia's green gaze chided him for abandoning her.

Bella gave him an arch look before she closed the door behind him.

Caleb sat in the waiting room thinking about how vulnerable Mia seemed seated in that big austere office. Only this morning he'd been planning to try to coerce her into offering money for Lily's care. He knew now that he wouldn't force her into anything.

That change of heart confused Caleb. But one thing was for sure. He might feel empathy for Mia, want to help—even rescue her, but he couldn't let any of those emotional responses sway his goal to obtain justice for Lily. She was the true innocent here. His concern for the lovely Mia, even though she'd been done wrong, could not affect his professional judgment. But why did God always allow the innocent to get hurt?

He texted his office for an update, glad to be away. Hours of fighting legal battles for clients who'd been wronged was the reason he'd chipped in for half the ranch with Lara. He'd seen it as a place to escape his work and since her death he'd been very grateful for the freedom it offered. His birth father's appearance in Buffalo Gap last week had made him even more grateful because too many angry memories from the past now assailed him. The only way Caleb could exorcise his loathing for the man was with long horseback rides into the hills. As a kid he'd always gone out there to clear his mind. Some things never changed.

Only now when he rode the ranch he saw Lara. Would he ever forget her last words to him?

You've let bitterness take over your world so much, I think it's wiped out your ability to love, Caleb. All I can feel is your hate for your father. It's consuming you. Deepening our relationship with your hate for him between us isn't going to work. You need to let forgiveness heal your heart before we can talk about a future together.

Forgiveness? Impossible when Caleb couldn't rid his mind of the image of his father shoving his mom and her falling backward down the stairs. That was his last memory of her. An hour later she was dead, and his world had never been the same. Sometimes late at night, alone on the ranch, he could still hear her telling him about God, how He loved Caleb, how they had to forgive his drunken father as God forgave them.

Caleb couldn't do it. How did a man who killed his wife deserve forgiveness? How could God forgive a sin like that? It didn't matter that scripture insisted that God forgave no matter what. Caleb couldn't forgive. That inability to reconcile with God ate at his soul like an acid that left only bitter wounds in its place.

His past drove Caleb to go beyond mere duty to ensure every child from Family Ties went to a home where love ruled. That was also what compelled him to find justice for sweet Lily, a delightful child whose father never bothered to know her. How could God forgive that?

Caleb's phone chimed. He read the texted answer to his last question, then sent another. The stream of responses piqued his interest. Bella might try to shut him out of Mia's affairs, but Caleb had contacts. He intended to use every one to find out the truth, because somewhere in this mess was Lily's birthright.

"I can go now."

Caleb looked up from his phone, surprised to see Mia standing in front of him. They walked to his car in relative silence, but once they were inside, the intensity of her clear green gaze focused on him.

"Thank you for taking me to Bella. She's quite a character." Mia continued to study him. "Is it rude to ask how you met?"

"I was her law clerk. She taught me a lot." Caleb started the car before realizing he didn't know where to take her. "Do you want to go home?"

"I suppose so." The way Mia said it made Caleb think she did not relish a return to her dowdy home.

"What *would* you like to do?" he asked, curious about her thoughts. She looked slightly dazed, but then who wouldn't after hearing they had a trust fund they'd never heard of, that her husband had betrayed her and that he'd left behind a child?

And that wasn't even mentioning the attempt to steal her inheritance, information that had just been confirmed.

"It's kind of you, but I don't want to take up any more of your time," Mia said after a tiny hesitation. "I can take the bus from here. You don't have to drive me home."

"I don't have to, no." Caleb could see there was something on her mind. "I'm offering. Is there something else you'd like to do?"

"Yes." The response spilled out in a rush. "I'd like to see this Riverbend Ranch you mentioned." Her eyes softened to misty green. "A ride out of the city would be lovely. Space, freedom, nothing but green grass, hills and trees—it's been so long since I've been away from home." The light in her eyes faded. "But that's too much to ask."

"The place is yours. You should see it." Caleb felt a smug satisfaction saying that. He wanted to be the one to show Mia Riverbend Ranch, to watch her eyes stretch wide with wonder, hear her breathy gasp when they drove up the circular driveway. Somehow he knew that Mia would appreciate everything about the ranch.

"Of all the things Bella explained to me, I understand this ranch business the least. Why would Harlan buy such a place and keep it a secret from me?" Her voice quavered. "I must have done something."

"No. You did nothing, Mia." Caleb clenched his hands on the wheel, wishing he had more to offer than paltry words to soothe her wounded heart. "It was Harlan. There was something wrong with him that made him go outside his marriage for companionship."

"I can't understand that, either. You're sure he and Reba—?" Her tone told him she wanted it to be otherwise.

"I'm pretty sure. You saw the resemblance for yourself." Caleb hated saying it, hated the hurt filling her eyes and the wash of tears. But he'd feel bad for any woman in this situation. "I'm sorry."

"Our marriage was a sham." Mia choked out the words. "I'd accepted that it was only because of my mother that he married me, but now I suspect he really married me to get her money."

"Yes," Caleb agreed.

"We had nothing in common. Harlan didn't care about God or keeping His commandments, but this is so far from—" For a few moments she gave way to bitter tears.

Caleb wanted to fold her in his arms and soothe her, but that wouldn't be proper. He barely knew Mia and yet he longed to make her world right? Silly and impossible. His own past had taught him that nothing could erase the betrayal she must be feeling. So he let her cry, knowing she needed the release.

"You said Lily is five?" Mia hiccuped a sob. "That means they've been together about as long as we've been married. Why stay married to me if he was in love with Reba?" She dashed a tear from her cheek. "Why not marry her? Create a family with her?"

"There's no way you'll ever know." Caleb refused to restate the obvious lure of her money. He wasn't sure she had an inkling of how much her mother had left her, but his sources told him the number was high, very high.

"He knew how much I love children," Mia said on a sob. "I would have liked to meet Lily." Suddenly she gulped and her eyes went dead. "I guess he thought I'd hurt—"

Caleb waited, curious about the comment.

Mia paused, licked her lips, then continued in a quieter voice, "Harlan said he never wanted to have children."

"Judging by the amount of attention he paid Lily, I'm guessing that part was true." Caleb frowned. *I'd hurt—?* Mia wouldn't hurt a flea. He knew that for certain, though how he knew it was a question he'd ask himself later.

"If he didn't want a child, then why—?" Her wounded voice died away.

"Maybe it was Reba's idea. Maybe she hoped having Lily would solidify their relationship. Or maybe Lily was an accident." He wanted to lift Mia's spirits and wondered why it seemed so important to do that.

"I don't believe any child is ever an accident," Mia said firmly. "Every birth is a promise from

God. I wish—I wish I could have a child." She began to weep as though her heart was broken.

Caleb watched helplessly, thinking what a wonderful mother this caring woman would make. Somehow he knew that Mia was cut from the same cloth as his mother had been. Mia would welcome a child, make it feel loved, the most important person in her world. Mia would intrinsically know how and when to give a hug. Things Caleb lacked. Because of his father.

"May I give you some advice?" he asked when he couldn't stand to watch her weep any longer.

"Of course." Mia blinked away her sadness. Hope fluttered in its place.

"Harlan betrayed you. There's nothing you can do about that. But he's gone." How odd it was to advise Mia to do what he couldn't. "I'm sure you did your best to be his wife, but now you have to forget all the whys of the past and move on to what's next."

"What is next?" She frowned at him. "I doubt anything's truly changed. I'll continue designing. I like doing that. Maybe I'll have some repairs done on the house if I can afford it."

"Is that all?" Frustrated by her simple response, Caleb wanted Mia to widen her horizons, to think about the possibilities that could fill her life now.

"That's quite a lot for me, actually," Mia said pertly.

"But you could do much more." Caleb turned

off the highway toward Buffalo Gap and River-bend Ranch. "You have opportunities now, Mia. You should take advantage of them." When she didn't immediately answer he glanced her way and found her studying him, a pensive look on her face.

"Opportunities like what?" she asked.

"Do you drive?"

"No. I don't know how." She shook her head, her amazing hair trembling with the motion. "My mother wasn't in favor of me learning."

"You were only seventeen then," he reminded her. "Your mother probably thought she'd get you lessons later."

"Maybe. Harlan didn't want me to drive," she said thoughtfully.

Caleb wasn't surprised by that. Freedom to drive anywhere meant Harlan risked Mia seeing him with Reba.

"Why did you ask?" She studied him, her head tilted to one side.

"Wouldn't now be a good time to take driving lessons? When you get your driver's license you can buy a car." Caleb watched her eyes flare, heard her gasp.

"I can't afford a car!"

"I think if you ask Bella she'll tell you that you can afford to buy a car," he said, hiding his smile. So she still didn't know. "Maybe two of them."

"Why would I need two cars?" Though Mia

frowned at him, she was clearly captivated by the possibility of learning to drive wherever she wanted to go. "I suppose I could learn to drive Harlan's car, though it's very big and fancy. I wouldn't want fancy. I might ruin it."

"A car can be fixed," Caleb said, irritated that Mia was so willing to deny herself a simple thing that would bring her freedom. "If you like trees and open spaces, you should consider moving to the ranch."

"I couldn't do that." Mia looked shocked by the idea. "It's not mine."

"It will be." He took pity on her confusion. "I did some investigating. I was trying to figure out how to get some money for Lily from Harlan's estate."

"Oh." Mia frowned at him, obviously troubled by his admission.

"I learned that the ranch is fully paid for. There is no mortgage or lien on it. Harlan is listed as the sole owner, so it will pass to you." He paused for a moment. "If you lived there, you could have Lily visit." He let out his pent-up breath, hoping she wouldn't be repulsed by the idea of seeing her husband's child.

"No, I couldn't. I could never have Lily visit," Mia said in a very firm tone.

Caleb stared, surprised by how adamant she sounded. He didn't ask why. Mia's world had already been turned upside down. He didn't want to add to that now.

"Anyway, I thought you said she was being adopted?" she added.

"Actually, I didn't say that. Abby Lebret runs Family Ties. She's the one who will find Lily a home," he said in his most calming tone. "I'm just trying to help. Don't worry. Sooner or later Lily will have a family."

"Everything is such a whorl." Her confusion tugged at him. "Nothing is what I believed it to be, especially Harlan having an affair." She blinked furiously. "I didn't see that coming."

"Because he didn't want you to. Because you trusted him," Caleb said. How could he have ever thought her capable of dissembling? "Don't blame yourself. I'm sure he went to great lengths to make sure you didn't suspect him."

"Proof that I've been living in a fairy world." Mia blew out a sigh that ruffled the hairs across her brow. "I feel like Alice in Wonderland after she fell down the rabbit hole. Everything is bewildering." Fear crept across her face. "I should go home and wait until it's all sorted out."

"You can't run away from the truth, Mia." Caleb's heart ached for her. It had to be horribly confusing to have your entire world turned upside down. "This is just a visit. You don't have to decide anything. You're only going to take a look at Riverbend."

"I guess." Mia gazed out the window with appreciation, repeatedly commenting on the glorious colors of the hillside foliage. "I wish I had my camera," she said wistfully. "I'll never remember these exact shades of red and orange."

"Why do you need to?" Then Caleb remembered her paintings. "You can use my phone," he offered, pulling to the side of the road. "I'll email the pictures to you. You do have email?" he asked as an afterthought.

"Of course. I have to. That's how I connect with my employers." Mia's impish grin made his heart rate pick up. "I don't live completely in the Dark Ages, you know."

"I never said—" Caleb took a second look at her face and chuckled. When he'd first met Mia he never expected her to be such a delight.

One that he wanted to know much better.

"I've probably drained your battery and clogged up your data space with all my pictures," Mia said as she handed over Caleb's phone. "But I just can't get enough of these colors."

"How will you transfer them to fabric?" he asked as he helped her back into his car.

"I'm not sure I can." She smiled, feeling more carefree than she had felt in ages. "But I have to try. Those brilliant reds and oranges would make wonderful quilts combined with leafy greens and silvers, and those subtle shades of browns. Maybe if I—"

Realizing she was chattering, Mia went quiet, pretending to ignore Caleb's searching look. He was a nice man, sometimes gruff and grouchy, but she was fairly certain that was a mask to hide his soft inside. She knew no one else who would have dived into her affairs, helped her find a lawyer and then taken her for this ride. With every mile her questions about Caleb Grant grew.

Suddenly Mia's mind went blank as a lovely log home appeared before her, two stories with fence-post railings and a swing on the deck that exactly matched one she'd dreamed about in the days when dreams still seemed possible.

"Welcome to Riverbend Ranch," Caleb said. She felt his stare even though she wasn't looking at him.

"It's so beautiful." Mia gaped at the magnificent house. Set against a stand of dark green evergreens, the log home stood proudly, waiting to welcome whoever stepped through the massive door. She could feel its warmth and hospitality drawing her from here.

"Come on." Caleb waited for her to exit the car, then shoved the door and grabbed her hand. "Let's explore."

Walking beside him, Mia felt funny, odd and yet somehow wonderful with her hand dwarfed in his. Tall, strong, dependable Caleb. Though leery of trusting anyone, she somehow felt Caleb Grant was the kind of man you could always depend on. Still, mistrust had taken root in the past few hours. She wasn't going to depend on Caleb for anything more than some help.

"I grew up in a house like this." He paused to gaze at the structure. "My parents still live there. I'll take you to meet them sometime."

Questions about Caleb's family multiplied. Maybe someday she'd know him well enough to ask them. Her thoughts scattered at the sight of the roses climbing the railings.

"Aren't they glorious?" Mia let go of his hand because his touch made her stomach woozy. She bent to inhale the scent of the whitest bloom. "Persians always smell the best."

"You know roses?" Caleb looked surprised.

"I grow them in my back garden, though never as big as these." She climbed the three front steps, turned and took in the view. "I can see for miles. So beautiful yet so odd."

"Why odd?" Caleb sank down on one of the rockers.

"Harlan hated the outdoors, animals, anything not city. He liked sleek and modern, not oldie moldy, as he called it." She shrugged. "Maybe he bought this place for Reba." She turned to look at him. "Do you think so?"

"Why would he? Reba had a condo in Calgary. Besides, her name isn't on the deed, only his. And he's owned this place for several years." He voiced his theory. "For the past three years there's been an upswing in ranch sales around Buffalo Gap. I wonder if he hoped to resell this place for a nice profit over what he paid for it."

Mia waited, realizing Caleb had something else to say.

"The local real estate agent commented that Harlan never went inside. She said he had a sheaf of papers. He walked the property while consulting his papers, then told her he'd take it."

"Like I said—it's odd." Knowing Harlan hadn't been inside made it easier for Mia to look through the windows. She gasped at the huge stone fireplace covering the end of one wall, a beautiful chandelier that sparkled in the sunlight and a lovely circular staircase. Suddenly conscious of how nosy she must seem, she backed away. "Excuse me," she said, her cheeks burning.

"Why?" Caleb shrugged. "Don't you want a closer look inside?"

Startled, she whirled around and asked, "Can we?"

"While you were soaking in the autumn colors I texted the caregiver and asked her to unlock it." Caleb turned the knob, pushed the door open and waved a hand for her to enter.

"That was kind of you." Mia walked past him, heart thudding. Caleb Grant *was* a very kind man, and very handsome, and very… Forcing her focus off him, she glanced around as the warmth of the house enfolded her like a comfortable quilt.

"Do you like it?" Caleb asked quietly.

"Who wouldn't? This is what a real home feels like." Mia ran her hands along a log, reveling in its satin smoothness. She gazed up at the vaulted ceiling. "The details are spectacular."

"It's big, I'll say that." Caleb strolled through the front room into a dining room and then the kitchen. Mia followed him, mentally placing her few precious items here and there. "Like it?" he asked, stopping in the kitchen.

"What's not to like?" The big sunny room overlooked a backyard with a screened gazebo, a fountain and a child's play set—for Lily, the child Harlan never wanted? The child she could never have. That hurt too much so Mia refocused. "The patio has a place for campfires and picnics." Her mind immediately began envisioning a fall campfire and the scent of burning leaves.

"Look at this room." Realizing Caleb had moved on, Mia followed his voice. "I think it's a family room, but the windows give it amazing light. You could paint in here."

"Plus, there's another fireplace to make it cozy." Riverbend was like the house Mia had once cut out of a magazine and dreamed of ever since, though she'd never dared pray for it. That was too much to ask when she didn't have anyone to share it with, not even a husband now. "It's a family home."

"It could be." Caleb insisted she inspect the four upstairs bedrooms. Each boasted a fantastic view. "It's a nice place," he said when they returned to the front porch.

"Nice?" His simple words jerked Mia from her bemusement. She sat on the porch swing and used her toe to push back and forth. "It's amazing. But I can't understand why Harlan bought it. It's not his type of home at all." She glanced at Caleb and felt her cheeks burn. "At least I didn't *think* it was. I guess I didn't really know him at all."

"Forget Harlan. I'm starving. Let's go have lunch." A moment later they were heading down a gravel road into town. Caleb pointed out different houses and named neighbors. "I live about four miles in that direction," he said, pointing.

"On a ranch." Mia heard the squeak in her own voice. Caleb must have heard it, too, but he simply nodded. "I didn't think of you as a rancher," she said. "I guess that makes me a bad judge of character again."

"Actually you're right. I'm not a rancher." He didn't look at her as he said, "I bought the ranch with a friend, as a sort of investment. Lara was Reba's sister."

Mia jerked upright, surprised he'd known Harper's secretary. Some suspicious gremlin in her head warned that Caleb was still a stranger.

"Lara was a veterinarian. The ranch was to be a refuge for injured or displaced animals."

"It's not that now?" Mia asked, sensing something had saddened him.

"It was Lara's dream. I've tried to keep her dream going, but I'm failing. I finally took my mom's advice and listed the place last week." Caleb pulled into a parking space in the small town. "Brewsters is a good place to eat," he said, his voice flat, emotionless.

Mia got out of the car, her mind trying to piece together the puzzle of Caleb Grant. This Lara must have been important to him. His voice had softened when he said her name, a trace of fondness lingering as he spoke of her.

Brewsters turned out to be a homey diner with tantalizing aromas filling the air. Most of the lunch crowd had left when a woman Caleb introduced as Paula Brewster greeted them and took their orders. Mia was about to sip her tea when an older woman bustled over and swallowed Caleb in a hug.

"You should have told me you'd be here, honey. I'd have changed my plans and shared lunch with you." The woman turned sharp inquisitive eyes on Mia. "Hello."

"This is Mia Granger, Mom. Mia, this is my mother and the town's mayor, Marsha Grant."

"Granger?" The woman frowned. "Any relation to Harlan Granger?"

"Mia was his wife." Caleb shook his head at his mother so subtly that Mia almost missed it. It seemed like a warning. "We were just looking at Riverbend."

"It's a gorgeous place. Too bad no one's living there. It needs a family." Marsha fluttered her hand at someone near the door. "I'd love to stay and visit, but I have a council meeting. Welcome to Buffalo Gap, Mia. I'm sorry about your husband, but I hope you come back again. Bye, dear." She brushed a kiss against Caleb's bristly cheek and then hurried away.

"Your mother seems very nice," Mia said politely.

"She's actually my foster mother and she is nice. Also nosy. I'll be inundated with questions about you later on." Caleb didn't seem worried. In fact, a small smile curved his lips.

Foster mother? Mia hesitated a moment, then asked, "Did your family have problems?"

"You could say that." His harsh laugh shocked her but not as much as his words. "My father murdered my mother. Marsha became my foster mother. She and her husband, Ben, later adopted me. Your mother made sure my father could never get custody of me again."

Caleb watched shock fill Mia's face and wondered why he'd felt the need to tell her the truth so harshly. His personal story was bad enough, but there was no need to couch it in such bitter terms, except that for the third time this week he'd just glimpsed his birth father here in Buffalo Gap, this time right across the street from Brewsters. In a flash the same old anger had bubbled up inside and splashed all over poor Mia.

"I'm sorry." Her lovely green eyes grew misty with suppressed emotion as she touched his hand in a brief gesture of sympathy. "That must have been very hard for you."

"I managed." No way was he going to dump the rest of his sordid life on her. "Marsha and Ben were a godsend. I even got a sister out of the deal. Cindy's a social worker in Calgary. She and Abby have worked together on several cases at Family Ties."

Their food arrived. Caleb dug into his soup and sandwich with gusto until he noticed Mia picking at hers.

"Is something wrong with it?" Feeling helpless at the sight of her tears, he said, "Mia—"

"I'm being silly." She sniffed and forced a smile. "It's just that I haven't eaten out in such a long time. Harlan said we had to save money—" He saw anger flash in those green eyes before she looked down. "Anyway, it's very nice of you to bring me here."

Caleb's heart pinched at those words. She was grateful for a meal out? It emphasized the solitary life Mia had led. How could Harlan Granger have treated this sweet woman so shabbily?

"Now I've ruined your lunch." She groaned. "I'm sorry."

"Nothing's ruined." He studied her for a moment. "I want to ask you something, Mia, but I don't know if I should."

Her smile flickered nervously. "What is it?"

"Since you're here in Buffalo Gap anyway, would you like to visit Lily?" Caleb held his breath as he waited for her answer.

"I don't know." Mia's fearful look returned.

"We wouldn't have to tell her exactly who you are," he reassured her. "It's just that with her mother gone she gets lonely and…" He let it trail away, knowing he was asking too much when Lily was her husband's child with another woman. "Never mind."

"Actually, I think I would like to see her, as long as you'll be there." Mia played with her teacup. "Maybe seeing her would bring some sense to this strange day."

"Great!" Caleb found himself grinning. "Lily's a sweet girl. This was Reba's hometown. She used to come back and visit Lara a lot, so folks in town got to know Lily. In fact, over the years almost everyone in town has taken a turn babysitting her."

"Even you?" Mia studied him from beneath her lashes.

"Even me," he agreed quietly, remembering the

fun times he and Lara had spent with Lily. "Her aunt and I used to date so Lily calls me her uncle."

"*Used to* date?" Mia stared at him, waiting.

"Lara died six months ago." He met her gaze and saw questions widening her eyes.

"Oh. Where does Lily live now?" He thought Mia played with her cup to hide her expressions.

"Officially I'm her guardian. Lara and Reba lost their parents years ago, so Lily's staying with a woman named Hilda Vermeer, a foster mother." He grimaced. "She was a real tartar when I was a kid, but she's mellowed a lot since. I think Lily feels safe with her."

"Children should feel safe," Mia murmured almost to herself.

"Your mother said that to me once." Caleb figured it was unlikely that Harlan would talk about his former partner. He thought Mia must feel starved for details about her mother. Again that desire to protect her bloomed inside him.

"She protected you from your father," Mia said thoughtfully. "Maybe that's why she arranged for me to marry Harlan, to keep me safe."

Not Pia's best decision, Caleb mused, *given the jerk Harlan turned out to be.*

"It's past three," he said after checking his watch. "Lily will be home from kindergarten. I could phone Hilda, ask her if we could come over." He waited, certain that if Lily and Mia could form a bond, chances were that Mia might agree to support Harlan's child and legal action against the estate wouldn't be necessary.

And you wouldn't feel so guilty for not adopting Lily yourself.

"I don't know." Hesitation was written all over her face. But something dark and fearful also lurked in her eyes, something Caleb didn't understand.

"It doesn't have to be a long visit," he encouraged. "I drop in to see her most days. You can say hello." She didn't look convinced, so he pushed harder. "Don't you want to see Harlan's child?"

"Yes, but—" A nerve ticked in her cheek "You don't understand." She glanced sideways at him, then sighed heavily. "Today has been full of surprises."

"I know. It hasn't been easy for you and this must have come as quite a shock. But surely meeting a five-year-old girl doesn't scare you." Caleb immediately regretted those words because it was clear Mia was panicking at meeting Lily. "I'll be right there," he soothed. "We can leave whenever you want."

That seemed to ease her fears. "You're sure?"

"It's just a meeting, that's all."

"As long as you stay. I can't be alone with her," Mia said, her voice raspy.

"Hilda and I will both be there." He smiled. "I'm so glad you're doing this. You'll love Lily."

Caleb made the call and after a few minutes' drive they were at Hilda's.

Caleb saw Mia's face soften when she caught sight of the little girl sitting in a corner of the porch. She studied Lily intensely, taking in every detail of her stepdaughter.

"Welcome. I've made us some iced tea. It's so lovely today we'll drink it on the porch," Hilda said after Caleb had introduced Mia.

He wasn't surprised to see Lily hang back. Since her mother's death she'd become unsure and tentative about most things. He hated the way the little girl clung to Hilda's skirt as if fearing she'd be abandoned again. Caleb knew he wasn't capable of giving her what she needed, but he had a hunch Mia could, *if* she would.

"Iced tea would be lovely. Thank you." Mia smiled. The warmth in her words reached Hilda's heart judging by Hilda's wide smile.

"Have a seat. It won't take me a minute." The older woman bustled inside.

Caleb knew Lily would have preferred to follow Hilda, but that would have meant walking in front of Mia, thereby revealing her damaged leg. He felt his heart squeeze with regret, saddened to see the formerly bubbly child now standing silent in the corner, dark blue eyes riveted on Mia. He struggled to find a conversation opener and came up blank.

"It's a lot of hair, isn't it?" Mia mused aloud,

reaching a hand to her head. Though she didn't actually look at Lily, it was obvious the child was the target of her remark. "Sometimes I wish it was shorter like yours. Your hair is so pretty. Those ribbons are perfect." Mia caught her own hair in her hand and tried to twist it into a ponytail like Lily's.

"You look like a clown." Lily promptly burst into the giggles.

"I know." Mia pulled out a small tablet and a pen from her purse and began sketching a clown with big curly hair, a bulbous red nose and striped balloon pants. "Like this?" she asked, holding out the pad.

Clever, Caleb silently applauded. Why had Mia been afraid when she was so obviously at ease with children?

Mia held the drawing so that Lily had to move nearer to get a good look, which meant she awkwardly shifted her leg. Mia didn't seem to notice. Instead, she kept drawing, adding to the sketch. In moments Lily was fully vested in the picture, pointing out areas that needed enhancement.

"Can you draw a dog, a brown one?" Lily asked.

"I'll try." Mia began sketching until under Lily's tutelage the face of a chocolate Lab appeared.

"It's perfect." Lily grinned. "That's the dog I want. And I'm going to call him Mr. Fudge."

"That's a great name," Mia said. "Who doesn't like fudge?"

The air left Caleb's chest in a rush of relief. This relationship was going to be a success. Mia would make it so because that was the kind of woman she was: caring, gentle and full of love just waiting to be expressed. Maybe her fear had to do with Lily's father, and yet he saw no fear in Mia now, just a sweet spirit that Lily was warming to. He'd been right to bring them together.

He studied the two heads, one so dark, one shimmering with light, just like her mother's. He had a hunch that Mia would one day make some lucky child an incredible mother. Some child— like Lily?

Caleb seldom prayed anymore. God seemed too far away. But this afternoon the soundless plea slipped from his heart.

Can You find Lily a new mom, God?

As Lily's giggles filled the air, Caleb couldn't think of anyone he'd rather see her with than sweet, gentle Mia.

Chapter Three

❧

"Lily's an incredible child." Mia couldn't conceal how moved she was after meeting her husband's daughter.

"You didn't feel a barrier because she's, well, your stepchild?"

"Not at all." Her certainty surprised Mia. "It's obvious Harlan was her father. Those eyes and that chin give it away, but Lily is her own person. She isn't responsible for Harlan's betrayal. She's just a little girl who's lost her mother."

"I'm glad you feel that way," Caleb said warmly. The admiration and appreciation in his gaze warmed a lonely place Mia always kept hidden.

Perhaps it also emboldened her because she blurted, "What happened to Lily's leg?"

"A riding accident." Caleb shuddered. "A year ago she was on a horse for the first time and it threw her. Lily broke her leg. It was a complicated break and hasn't healed well."

"Can it be fixed?" Mia asked.

"Reba told Lara she couldn't find a surgeon willing to try another operation." Caleb's forehead furrowed. "I haven't had time to check into that. Abby Lebret, the woman who runs Family Ties and is trying to find Lily a home, might have more information."

"Family Ties—oh, yes, the adoption agency you mentioned. So you've handed care of Lily over to them?" Mia said, not managing to hide her disapproval.

"It seemed best. I'm not father potential," he said, defensively, Mia thought.

"I thought you were very loving with her, exactly as a father would be." She mentally replayed her meeting with Lily. "She reminds me of myself at her age." She didn't realize she'd spoken her thoughts aloud until she heard Caleb's voice.

"How is that?"

"I was a sickly child. I missed a lot because I was often in hospital or at home recuperating." Wishing she'd kept silent and fearing Caleb would press to hear more, Mia explained, "It was hard socially when I joined school after the others had already made friends."

"You think Lily's missing out like that?" The idea seemed to startle him. "I've been so intent on getting her affairs worked out that I never gave much thought to her social state."

"She seems a bit restrained. That's probably due

to just losing her mother, but I have a feeling her leg also holds her back from being more outgoing." Mia shrugged. "I may be way off base. I'm not a child expert." She gave a harsh laugh. "Far from it, in fact."

"Actually you're right. Before the accident, Lily was bubbly, giggling all the time. You're the first one I've heard make her laugh in ages." His frown reappeared. "I should visit her more often. Maybe take her out so she doesn't brood. I'll have to do better."

Caleb's soft voice, his thoughtful words and the gentle goodbye kiss he'd brushed across Lily's cheek all revealed his soft spot for her. Mia found it indescribably attractive that this hard-nosed lawyer became putty in Lily's tiny hands.

"Thank you for taking me to meet her. She's a darling child. It's Harlan's loss that he didn't really know her." It was the first time she'd ever said anything negative about her husband, but after meeting Lily, Mia was annoyed that he'd apparently ignored the sweet little girl, his own daughter.

"You and she seemed to bond." Caleb's mild tone made her check his face. Nothing unusual there, but the way he'd said it, almost smugly…

"Who wouldn't bond with Lily?" Mia was immediately sorry she'd said that because they both knew Harlan hadn't bonded with her. "I wish you the best in finding her a new family to love her," she added, hoping to dissuade him from considering her as a candidate for Lily's mother.

"Thanks." Caleb fell silent.

Mia bit her lip. If Caleb knew about her past, the mistake she'd made that had cost a child his life—she refocused, saw his face alter into that blank-mask look he favored.

"So what's next for you, Mia?" he asked.

"That's the second time you've asked me that question." Wondering at the reason for his query, Mia searched his face for a clue. "Why?"

"Just wondering if you'd come and visit her again," he said.

Visiting Lily alone was the *last* thing she could do.

"I have no way to get out here. I don't drive, remember?" The joke fell flat when Caleb suddenly slowed and turned right. "Wh-where are we going?"

"To do some driver training." He flashed a grin before pulling onto a seldom-used gravel road. "Ready?"

"I can't—" Mia gulped, then swallowed her words when he jumped out of the car. When he opened her door, she reminded him, "I don't have a permit."

"We'll rectify that later. This is my land, so right now you're perfectly legal to drive on it since I'm with you. Trust me. I'm a lawyer." He gave her a cheeky grin. "If you get into trouble, I'll bail you out, or sweet-talk the cops."

Trust wasn't something Mia was ready to give, but what choice did she have?

"You may regret this," she advised. When it became clear he wasn't backing down, she sighed her resignation, walked around the car and climbed in on the driver's side. "Fasten your seat belt," she ordered as if she knew what she was doing.

Caleb obeyed with a deep-throated chuckle. "Yes, ma'am."

"Now what?" She prayed she didn't ruin his vehicle. It looked expensive. She flicked the key as told and flinched when the motor ground too long.

"Twist, then let go," Caleb directed calmly. Mia repeated the action with better results. "Good. Now you need to start moving. Right pedal is the gas." He waited for her nod. "Left is the brake. Keep your foot on that while you put the car into gear and then *gently* press on the gas pedal."

Mia followed his words and gave a little squeal when the car started rolling forward. She froze, her fingers clinging to the wheel as the car headed for the ditch.

"You do have to steer," Caleb said in a mild tone as he turned the wheel so the car returned to the middle of the road. "Don't worry about oncoming traffic. I'm the only one who lives on this road. I moved out here after Lara died."

It took all Mia's concentration to keep the car

wanted to do. It feels as if any change I make would be like killing her dream. I can't do that, either." He stared through the windshield. His next words were reflective. "I guess I've finally realized that what was her dream isn't what I want in my future. I have to move on."

"Sometimes that's a hard thing to accept." Mia looked at her hands as she remembered the many times she'd tried to learn what drove Harlan so she could become part of his life. And failed.

They rode for a while until Caleb broke the silence.

"You have an amazing talent for drawing. Did your mother approve?"

"She never said." Mia smiled in reminiscence. "But whenever she found me sketching she'd say something like, 'It's good you can amuse yourself.' I don't know what she'd think of my quilt designs now. The law was what she lived for."

"Was she a godly woman?" Caleb asked as he turned up her street.

"She had faith, though she wasn't showy about it. She used to take me to church when I was little. Sunday morning at church was one thing we did together." Mia pushed away the sad thought that now she had nobody in her life. "I think she felt brain cancer was the worst trick God could play on her. She couldn't stand the idea that she would lose her faculties."

"I can understand that," Caleb said.

"She took too much morphine and died in her sleep." Mia paused, then whispered, "I always wondered if she did that intentionally to avoid losing control." She felt Caleb's start of surprise before he braked in front of her house.

"I'm sure it wasn't deliberate. Pia was too strong to take the easy way out." His words sounded soothing, gentle.

"The doctors said the same, but sometimes I still wonder." Mia liked the way Caleb looked directly at her. So many people never made eye contact. "My mother consulted with a minister before she died. Later he told me she had a lot of questions for God."

"I hear that." There was a tightness in Caleb's voice that intrigued Mia. "I have a lot of questions for Him myself."

"You?" She hadn't considered this competent man would question anything.

"Sure. As a kid I wondered why He'd placed me in the home He had, why my mother died as she did, why my father never went to prison." He made a face. "I'm still asking that last one today. It drives me nuts to see him walking free around Buffalo Gap."

Mia's sympathy welled for the young Caleb who'd lost his beloved mother. "He's contacted you?"

"He's tried, but I don't want anything to do with Joel Crane. Ever." As if to end the discussion Caleb got out of the car and walked around to open her door. "It's been a pleasure meeting you, Mia Granger," he said as they walked to her front door.

"You, also, Caleb Grant." So he'd divested himself of the name Crane. Interesting. "It seems as if I've known you more than a single day." She pulled out her key and unlocked the door. "Thank you for everything you've done. I don't know where I'd have been if you hadn't come along."

"Will you be all right now?"

How could she have thought his eyes hard? They glowed now like warm molten silver, chasing away the late afternoon's chill.

"I'm always all right." Mia forced a smile she didn't feel. "I have to be. I'm the only one I have."

"You can call me if you need me." Caleb handed her a business card. "In fact, let's keep in touch."

"I'd like that," she said, and meant it. "Thank you for everything you've done."

"Make sure you get in touch with a driving school," he said. The wink he shot her way made her blush. "You've started now. There's no going back."

Mia's shyness returned full force. She wanted to escape, to be alone while she pondered everything about this unusual day, but especially about this kind, determined, gentle man. She enjoyed his presence in her world very much—because he made her think about the future and not the past?

"No, there is no going back," she repeated. "Goodbye, Caleb."

He nodded. "See you."

As Mia watched him walk down her garden path, she wondered if she'd ever see Caleb again. He'd been so nice to her, saving her from Trent, helping her find Bella, buying her lunch, taking her to see Riverbend Ranch and to meet Lily. It made her realize how lonely she was.

It also made her realize how hungry she was for the companionship he offered. If only her mother had chosen someone like Caleb instead of Harlan… But no, she couldn't think that way. God had a reason for directing things as He had. Still, the only thing her marriage had left her with was a firm determination never to trust anyone again.

Not that she had to worry, Mia decided as she went inside. Caleb was just being nice to her because he wanted money for Lily. He'd been very clear about that.

Why did that make her sad?

"Forgiveness isn't something we get to choose, nor can we ignore it simply because forgiving is hard or because it seems too onerous," Pastor Don said in his Sunday-morning message. "God *commands* us to forgive."

Caleb shifted uncomfortably. He felt as if the minister had seen him glimpse over one shoulder, observed his angry jerk of surprise at the sight of Joel in the back row, head bowed, pretending piousness. Why was he here? What did he want?

Didn't matter, Caleb decided. Nothing was going to change. If not forgiving was wrong, then he'd just have to deal with God's punishment because there was no way Caleb could stop blaming his father for his mother's death.

When the service was over, Caleb left as quickly as he could, preferring to skip the fellowship potluck dinner so he wouldn't encounter his father. He went home, scrounged together a sandwich for lunch and considered a ride into the hills. But he'd sold Lara's horses. When he couldn't seem to settle on any specific task, he climbed into his vehicle and went for a drive, surprised to realize he was heading toward Calgary.

To see my sister, he mused. His brain scoffed. *To see Mia.*

The image of her lovely face framed by that mass of golden-red curls filled his mind. What was it about her he found so attractive? Her jaunty spirit that refused to be quelled even though she'd been betrayed in the worst possible way? Her tender kindness toward Lily? Her faith in God? All of those, he decided. And more.

At first Caleb had thought Mia too passive, but he'd begun to understand that her hesitation wasn't always due to fear, but more often because she simply didn't know the next step. Yet even with that excuse, he'd been unable to shake the look on her face or her words about being alone with Lily. She'd been afraid, truly afraid, and he couldn't stop wondering why. Had her marriage not been platonic, as he'd assumed? Had she lost a child?

Some inner imp compelled him to turn down Mia's street. Caleb only intended to drive past her house, but before he arrived there he spotted her walking briskly toward him. What else could he do but pull up beside her and roll down his window?

"Want a ride?"

"Hello, Caleb." A smile stretched across Mia's pretty face as the wind caught her glorious hair and tossed it back. "What are you doing here?"

"Out for a Sunday drive. Get in." The genuine pleasure glinting in her green eyes sent a surge of warmth through him that chased away his anger at his father. He waited till she was belted in, then drove the short distance to her home. "How are you, Mia?"

"Doing well. I had a good talk with my pastor and with Bella, which helped clarify some of the issues I've been struggling with." She turned to study him. "And you?"

"Feeling guilty." Seeing her puzzled look, he smiled. "Today's sermon was about forgiveness. My father was there."

"Ah." He liked the way she said nothing more. She waited till he'd parked, then asked, "Are you coming inside?"

"I won't be in the way?" Caleb asked, only then realizing she might have something planned for her day.

"Of course not." She made a face. "I was going to offer you tea, but after the last time—say, why didn't you get sick?"

"I never drank it. Can't stand the stuff." He made a goofy face.

"But your cup was empty."

"I emptied it." He smiled when Mia shot him a quizzical look. "Have you noticed your plants by the table suffering any ill effects?"

"One of them has wilted. I wondered why." Mia's merry chuckle echoed in the crisp autumn air as she preceded him up the walk. She opened the door and waited for him to enter. "By the way, I received your letter requesting a meeting about Lily. Bella said it was in with a bunch of stuff Trent had."

"Oh." So she hadn't ignored him, Caleb mused. Mia hadn't even seen his letter when he first visited.

"Bella says you want money from Harlan's estate for Lily." She looked directly at him. "But I already knew that."

"I think Lily, as Harlan's daughter, is owed something." Relief that it was out in the open surged through Caleb.

"I do, too, but Bella says I'm not supposed to tell you that. Not yet anyway." She hung up her jacket and his, then led the way to the kitchen. "Have you had lunch?"

"Sort of." He grinned. "Peanut butter and dill pickle sandwich. It's all I had in the fridge."

"Is that good?" Mia asked curiously. When he nodded she said, "I'll have to try it sometime, but for lunch today I'm longing for pizza. Will you share it with me?"

"Sounds great." He sat down at the kitchen table and blinked in surprise when Mia set a knife and a cutting board in front of him. "What's this?"

"You didn't think you'd eat free, did you?" she teased. "You can cut up the pineapple and vegetables."

"You're going to *make* a pizza," he said, finally tweaking to her plan. "*Homemade* pizza?"

"I won't poison you," she promised, and giggled at his eye rolling. "I promise."

They worked together companionably, her mixing and rolling out her dough, him cutting up whatever she handed him. The tiny, dingy kitchen felt comfortable to Caleb in a way that his own high-priced stainless-steel one did not, but he was fairly certain that was because of Mia and not the appliances. She hummed softly as she worked.

"That's a tune from *The Nutcracker*," he said, recognizing the notes. "I heard it often when I was growing up because my sister was usually the Sugar Plum Fairy in her ballet class."

"It's always been my favorite ballet." Mia took

a quick look at him, then went back to kneading. "It's so full of hope and a child's joy. I go to see that ballet every New Year's Eve. It's my way of celebrating a new beginning."

Mia went to the ballet by herself on New Year's, a time when most couples made it a point to be together, to start the year with a kiss. Caleb's heart winced at the loneliness she must have endured. But beneath that curiosity grew. What would it be like to kiss Mia?

"I've never been to a real ballet," he said to chase away his wayward thoughts.

"You should go." Mia smoothed tomato sauce over her crust, then added all the bits he'd chopped topped by cheese. She slid it into the oven and washed her hands. She seemed nervous. Caleb wondered why until she said, "Can I ask you something?"

"Sure." He waited.

"Why is it so important for you to get money for Lily?" The words rushed out, as if she'd been thinking of them for a while. "I mean, what is she to you?

"I've known Lily, through Lara, for a long time. Besides being her guardian, I'm like her uncle. And she's a child in need. I'd do the same for any of the kids that come through Family Ties," he said. "But you're right. There's something about Lily that compels me to go the extra mile to be certain she's provided for. Maybe it's because she's so alone. She has no home, no family and no support."

"But surely a child her age doesn't need much money." A frown marred Mia's beauty. "She needs love and care, a family, a home. Not a lot of money. At least not yet."

"It's about more than the money." Caleb didn't want to hurt her but he had to tell the truth, so he set his jaw and laid out the hard, cold facts. "It's *Harlan's* money I want, because he never acknowledged Lily as his daughter, never saw her as far as I know and never interacted with her."

"You mean he cheated her of a father, so you want him to pay," Mia said thoughtfully.

"Yes." Caleb reined in his temper. "I'm guessing he didn't provide for her in his will?" He waited a moment before adding, "Or for Reba, either."

"There's no mention of them," Mia confirmed quietly.

A second look at her face made Caleb take a wild shot. "Or you?"

"No. The will is dated long before we were married. There are no benefactors named. Bella said some things will come to me automatically. Everything else will be dispersed from the estate to me because I was married to him." She said it self-consciously, as if she was embarrassed to get what Harlan had owned.

"Your husband's lack of provision for you, his

wife, and for his own daughter really annoys me." Caleb accepted the plate she handed him. "But I'm also concerned because I've just learned there's a chance Lily could get specialized treatment for her leg. There will be costs attached."

"Of course," Mia murmured.

"Then later on she might want to go to college or start a business," he continued. "I think she should have money for her future, money that her father should have provided."

"That makes sense." Mia looked at him for several long moments as if assessing his words. She only broke contact when the oven timer dinged. "I guess it's ready."

Caleb watched her set the browned pizza on a table mat. She cut it deftly, slid a lifter under the golden crust and served them each a piece. She brought a pitcher of lemonade to the table and two glasses, then took her seat. She bowed her head and offered a short prayer over the food. When she lifted her head her green eyes met his, wide and clear.

"Let's eat," she said with a smile.

So they did.

"I can't get over how good this tastes," Caleb said for the third time. "You're an amazing cook."

"Thank you." She smiled as she served him the last slice of the pie. "You'd better savor this because I only have a slice of dried-up chocolate cake for dessert."

"Oh, dessert is going to be on me." Caleb left her to guess what that meant as he ate the last slice while Mia restored everything to pristine order. She caught his stare and blushed.

"Harlan hated a mess," she murmured. "I guess I've gotten into the habit—" Her eyes widened when he reached out and tugged on the perfectly straight tea towels that hung from the oven bar, making their hems hang crookedly.

"I saw that in a movie once." He grinned at her, delighted by the burst of musical laughter she couldn't stifle. "Come on. I'm taking you to my favorite dessert place in this town." He held out her jacket, waited for her to slip it on then led the way to his car. "I don't know why, but I somehow thought you'd have a cat," he mused as he drove downtown.

"I'd love a cat, but Harlan is—was allergic." Her eyes grew round. "I guess I could have one now," she said slowly.

"I guess you could." He grinned as he drove, pleased that she was finally seeing possibilities in her future. "What about driving lessons?"

"I've had two already." She grinned. "The first one was such a disaster that the instructor didn't even show up the second time. They sent someone else. He was an excellent teacher. Patient. Kind of like you," she said with a wink. "I'm to take a third lesson tomorrow."

"Good for you." A tug of pure satisfaction filled

Caleb. Mia was finally breaking free. He pulled up in front of his favorite ice cream shop. "Your choice. My treat."

"I haven't had ice cream in years." Mia licked her lips as she stood beside him and surveyed the many flavors listed in the window. "Harlan didn't—" She gave a tiny shake of her head and then said, "There are too many choices."

"Over fifty. Do not pick vanilla," he ordered with a pretend glower.

It took a while, but finally Mia chose pistachio. Caleb picked his favorite double chocolate chunk. Cones in hand, they wandered across the road to a small park to enjoy their treat. Mia pointed out the different species of trees and told him which would lose their leaves first.

"You know a lot about trees," Caleb said, secretly impressed by her knowledge. "You could put that to good use at Riverbend Ranch. The back garden needs some care," he hinted, delighted when a rush of excitement lit up her face.

"I love that house. There's lots of space to grow fresh vegetables." Her face took on a faraway look. "Maybe I could add a fruit tree or two."

"Sounds as if you've already moved in," he said.

"I wish I could." She nodded at his surprised look. "I'm serious. I'd love to have that home, though it would mean giving up my church and the convenience of the city."

"There's a very good church in Buffalo Gap," he said, secretly pleased she was talking about a move closer to Lily. "And we have grocery and hardware stores. But if you need something in the city, Calgary's only half an hour away."

"I'm aware of that." Her eyes strayed from him. Her face became pensive.

"What's holding you back?" he asked.

"Bella hasn't got everything straightened out yet," she said. "But if I did move to Riverbend, the one thing I can't escape is that it's a ranch. I have no idea what to do with a ranch, Caleb, no clue how to manage it or what needs to be done."

"So you hire someone to do the handiwork." He saw Mia wasn't convinced. "My mom said that most of the acres that go with the ranch have been rented to the neighbor for pasture for his horses. You could continue to do that."

"I didn't know that." Her face regained its excitement, sending his pulse thudding in response. "So I could live there with a little help for the odd jobs?"

"If you wanted." Caleb swallowed, deeply moved by the look of joy that filled her face. "It's simply a matter of making the decision and doing it."

"You have that philosophy about a lot of things, don't you?" Mia nodded, then licked her cone. "I guess I hesitate too much. I should adopt your approach and stop wavering."

Caleb finished his cone, torn between wanting to know her decision and feeling hesitant to press for an answer. Finally he could wait no longer.

"So leasing the extra land would make it possible for you to move to Riverbend Ranch?"

"Maybe." Mia's voice sounded stronger than he'd ever heard it. In fact, there was a new hint of self-confidence underlying her words that he found very attractive. "I'll have to talk to Bella, but one of these days Buffalo Gap might have a new resident in the community." She grinned at him. "You might have a new neighbor."

"Good," Caleb responded while his heart somersaulted at the prospect of having Mia nearby. Because of Lily, he told himself as they strolled through the park. He was glad because Mia would be nearer to Lily.

Naturally it was nice that Mia would also be close enough to drop in on occasionally. Just in case she needed him for something. But a friend was all Caleb would be to Mia. As Lara had pointed out, he didn't know how to love.

Chapter Four

"I'm glad you could come, though I'm sorry to bother you." A week had passed since Mia had seen Caleb. Now her heart danced as she opened the door wide to welcome him inside her home. "How are you?"

"I'm fine, thanks." Caleb's smile made his silvery eyes glow. To Mia, he looked very fine, but she couldn't let herself get sidetracked.

"Would you like some coffee?" she asked, leading the way into the kitchen.

"Coffee? You?" His silver eyes widened in disbelief. "I thought you were the original tea lady."

"I hope not original." Mia laughed as she turned to get the coffee, hoping to hide her blush. "I don't drink coffee, but I can certainly make it." She did so in the old-fashioned percolator she'd unearthed in the basement after she asked him to come.

"You don't want to sit in the sunroom?" Caleb shot a questioning glance at the closed door.

"It's usually too cool in the autumn without a lot of sun to heat it up," she explained.

"There's no heat?" He frowned when she shook her head. "But where do you work in winter?"

"In here or the living room," she said with a shrug. "When Harlan was alive I mostly waited to do my work until he wasn't here." She motioned to a chair and pulled out two mugs, hoping she could steer the conversation away from herself. "I hope you won't mind if I ask you some questions about Trent. Bella said you'd been investigating him?"

"Earlier this year on another case." Caleb eyed the pecan tarts eagerly. "Did you make these?"

"Yes. Help yourself," Mia invited. "We share coffee and munchies after Bible study. Tonight's my turn."

"I picked the right afternoon, then." Caleb selected a tart, took a bite and complimented her before asking, "What do you want to know about Trent?"

"I've been trying to understand why he would have tried to hurt me." Mia couldn't quite shake the sense of betrayal she still felt.

She felt Caleb hesitating, but then he said, "You can't know his motives, Mia. Maybe it was the money he watched Harlan take, maybe it was because he knew you'd never suspect him, maybe it was simply greed. I can tell you that suspicious circumstances around the deaths of his last two clients have the police investigating him."

"Oh, dear." She silently offered a prayer for others Trent might have hurt.

Caleb shrugged. "Something inside drove him. It's unlikely you'll ever discover what unless he talks, and I doubt his lawyer will allow that now."

Mia sighed, wishing his responses satisfied her.

"It's not really Trent you're asking about, though, is it?" Caleb said shrewdly, eyes narrowed. "I think you're really asking why *Harlan* did what he did. Am I right?"

"Yes." Mia struggled to quell a rush of tears, irritated that she couldn't shed these feelings of betrayal. "He stole from me. I can forgive that. But he cheated on me. Bella thinks he was probably having an affair even before we married. On top of which he had a child he never even mentioned."

"I'm sorry," Caleb offered quietly.

"Me, too." Mia couldn't hide her anger. Harlan's deceit ate at her like acid, especially because he of all people knew how desperately she longed to love a child and how she mourned the fact that she couldn't. "How am I supposed to understand what he did?"

"I know this is easy to say." Caleb exhaled, then said in a gentle tone, "You have to let it go. There's nothing you can do to change what happened or make it better or figure out why. It's nasty and dirty and hurtful, but all you can do now is move on."

"It's the scope of his betrayal I can't figure out.

Why not tell me straight out that he didn't want me, that I wasn't a good wife?" She bit her lip, embarrassed that she'd blurted that out. "Never mind."

Caleb's silence and the softening of his icy gaze made him look infinitely more approachable than the day she'd first met him, Mia decided. It also enhanced his good looks and that killer smile.

"Listen, Mia. It will take time, but you will get over those feelings." Caleb's hand rested on her shoulder in silent comfort, making her very aware of the intimacy building between them. Then he moved away and suddenly she could breathe again. "Were Trent and Harlan's actions the only reason you called me?"

Suddenly tongue-tied, Mia shook her head.

"Then?" He arched one eyebrow, chose another tart and waited while she refilled his coffee. When she was seated once more he leaned forward. "Tell me how I can help you."

"I want to do something with this house. Bella said you could advise me." She shifted under the intensity of his steely stare.

"You want my suggestion? Blow it up." He chuckled at her start of surprise. "Kidding. How can I advise you?"

"Give me the name of a good contractor." Mia saw Caleb's eyes flare as he glanced around the room. "I want to fix this house."

"So you're staying here." He sounded disappointed. "I can tell you that renovations will be expensive." He glanced around. "It looks to me as if there's been a lot of patchwork over the years. That's costly to remove. How far do you want to go?"

"As far as needed to make this a warm, comfortable, safe home." She hurried on before he could object. "I don't want there to be a single problem left, not to mention that I want it to look good."

"Repair the bathroom, gut the kitchen, heat for your solarium, to name a few." Caleb counted them off on his fingers as he spoke. "It's going to be quite a bill."

"I imagine so. But Bella says I have enough money to cover whatever expenses come up." Almost breathless at the possibilities, Mia waited. Somehow she knew Caleb wouldn't let her down. "Well?" she demanded impatiently when he didn't speak.

Mia couldn't explain it, but in that moment she felt as if a shield fell between them. He no longer studied her, but kept his gaze on a point just past her left ear.

"I thought you were considering a move to Riverbend," he said.

"Still am." Mia almost smiled when Caleb's eyes widened. She had a hunch the lawyer wasn't often surprised. "The renovations won't be for me, but there's no way I want to pass on all my problems for someone else to handle."

Was that admiration? A second later his stony lawyer face was back and Mia was left wondering if she'd imagined his approval. She must have. There was no way Caleb would care whether she moved to Riverbend or not.

"It's a good plan." He nodded. "You'd certainly get more money for the place."

"That's not my primary concern." Mia had to ask the question that had been bugging her. "Why did Bella tell me you'd be able to help?"

"She knows my past." Caleb smiled a funny sardonic grin. "I was working construction before she offered me a job. My foster father taught me a lot about building while I was growing up. I guess he thought I needed to pound something to alleviate my teenage frustration."

Mia smiled.

"It was easy for me to find work renovating and I needed the money to pay off my college loans. A law clerk doesn't make much and I didn't have the funds to start my own office then, so I did what I knew." Caleb shrugged. "I worked on Bella's office."

"It's lovely." She paused. "Your dad sounds like a great father." An angry look flashed across Caleb's face, puzzling Mia. "Wasn't he?"

"Ben was and is a fantastic father. I wish every kid could have a dad like him." The tribute flowed easily, but then Caleb's tone hardened. "As a father Ben is miles above the father I was born to."

"Oh, Caleb." Mia's heart squeezed with sympathy at the tight angry look on his face, but she had no idea how to ease it without prying. "Maybe your mother's death was a mistake and he's sorry it happened."

"I'm sure you're right." Caleb's lips compressed in a tight line. "Doesn't matter if he is. It doesn't change anything. He killed her."

"But he didn't go to prison," she said, trying to puzzle out details he hadn't shared.

"No. He got off." Those silver-gray eyes grew glacial. "I testified against him. Your mother prepared me, explained every step of it, over and over, to make sure the jury would hear what really happened. Pia was adamant that he not get away with murder."

"Yet the jury didn't convict." Mia knew very little about how the law worked, but she did know that her mother would have dotted every *i* and crossed every *t*. "What was the ruling?"

"Accidental death." He sneered. "They believed my father's story that Mom jerked away from him when he reached out and that's what caused her to fall backward down the stairs. She hit her head at the bottom and later died."

"I'm so sorry, Caleb." The bereft look on his face combined with the loss woven through his words gripped Mia's heart. What a horrible burden he carried. "Is it possible that is what happened? I mean, were you young enough that you might have misunderstood?"

"I was seven, but I didn't mistake anything, Mia. Every detail is still implanted right here." He tapped his temple. His voice hardened. "I can close my eyes and see it as clearly as if it happened five minutes ago. He was not innocent of her death."

"All right," she soothed as she searched for a different way to approach this. "But maybe he's sorry. Maybe he's found you because all he truly wants is your forgiveness."

"Well, he's not getting it." Ice dripped from the words. "Forgiveness is not something I can grant."

"Why?" she dared to ask, hiding the shudder that rippled through her when Caleb's glacial gaze turned on her.

"Because there are some things that cannot be forgiven." His cold, emotionless voice made her cringe.

"By you, you mean," she said in a quiet voice. "But God forgives."

"Some things not even He should forgive," Caleb snarled. "Killing my mother is one of them." He shook his head. "I don't want to talk about this anymore. What is it about this renovation that you need from me?"

"Names of people I should call." Mia stifled her concern for him and focused on her house.

"I don't know anything about renovations, so I'll have to depend on contractors who will tell me the truth, give me fair estimates and do the work properly. I should warn you, I don't trust easily."

"No wonder." Caleb sounded sympathetic, but the look on his face revived all the doubts she'd worked so hard to smother.

"Maybe I haven't thought this through enough," Mia murmured. "Maybe a renovation isn't something I should tackle."

"Chickening out already?" Caleb's grin chased the shadows from his face, though remnants lingered in the back of his cloudy eyes. "You'll need guidance, but there's no reason you can't renovate with the right people to help. You managed learning to drive."

"I did. With you cheering me on." She smiled, reveling in the knowledge that she was no longer utterly alone. Caleb would help her. "Can you do that again? Because I'm not sure I can handle this on my own."

"Why don't you walk me through the place so I can get a better idea of what's needed and who'd do the best job for you," Caleb said. "Can I borrow a notepad?"

"Sure." Mia grabbed her smallest sketch pad off the counter, flipped to a clean page and handed it to him. "Where should we start?"

"Let's go from bottom to top," Caleb suggested. He arched one eyebrow. "Basement?"

"This way. Watch your head. The steps are narrow." She felt embarrassed to let this man in his expensive clothes and shoes see her dingy basement, but at least his head wouldn't brush any cobwebs. She'd cleaned as best she could around Harlan's "leave alone" piles. At the bottom of the stairs she grimaced at the disorder.

"What's all this?" Caleb glanced at the stacks of boxes with a frown.

"It's—it was Harlan's. I wasn't allowed to look at it when he was alive. I'm still hesitant to go through his things." She shivered. "He was so adamant that I not touch these boxes. I only ever came down here to do laundry. I don't like it here."

"I wonder why?" he joked. "Dark, dank and dingy. Nobody's favorite place."

"I guess not." The boxes seemed to grow more intimidating until Caleb spoke.

"Do you mind if I glance through a couple of these so I know if they should be stored somewhere or hauled out as junk?"

"Go ahead." Rather him than her, but Mia couldn't keep herself from leaning forward as he opened the first box and pushed back a bunch of tissue. "What is it?" she asked when Caleb didn't move.

"Glass. Old, I think." Using a piece of tissue, he lifted a brilliant blue bowl from the box.

"It's beautiful, even in this dim light." Mia stared as the facets of the bowl caught the overhead light and sparkled even more. Her mind exploded with suspicion, but she masked her thoughts, silently searching the lines of the beautiful bowl for more clues.

"I wonder if all these boxes contain glass." Caleb stored the bowl carefully and moved on, checking through all the boxes. Finally he said, "Three boxes of glass, two of old papers and the rest look like old books."

"Harlan collected books." Mia suddenly remembered him once saying books were his best friends. "I should take them upstairs so I can go through them. I wouldn't want to take the chance of something being damaged by workmen."

But when she bent to lift one, Caleb stopped her.

"I'll do it," he said. "But first let's look around a bit more." He studied the mechanical area and scribbled some notes. "You need a new furnace. I'd also replace the water heater. You don't have air-conditioning?"

"I've often wished we had it in the sunroom," she said. "It's gets very hot in the summer."

"And cold the rest of the year," Caleb said. "A renovation is the time to remedy both. It's cheaper when all that work is done at one time." He surveyed the rest of the space.

Curious, Mia asked, "What are you thinking?"

"This space would make a great family room or kids' play area if it was finished."

"I can't see it," she said with a dubious shudder. "It's ugly down here."

"That could be changed," Caleb said. "Extra finished space would add to the value of the house. You should have plans drawn to see if it's something you want to do."

"Why?" She was intrigued by his vision of potential in this ugly place.

"Because it should be part of the renovation. It could be a great space." He saw her skepticism and grinned. "Trust me."

"I'm trying," she said, but a voice buried deep inside reminded her that she'd trusted two men and come to regret it. Caleb's eyes met hers and held. Something in the depths of those silver eyes made Mia shiver. "If you need to look more, go ahead. I'm going up."

"I'm finished here." He hefted the first box in his arms and followed her up the stairs. "Where shall I put this?"

"Here please. The others can go on the floor over there." Mia waited until Caleb had returned downstairs before she opened the box and lifted out the blue bowl. Lit by a spear of sunshine, it seemed to glow. Gently she turned it upside down and peered at the bottom. She caught her breath at what she saw.

"Anything good?" Caleb's voice startled Mia so that she lost her grip on the bowl. She froze as it flew downward. Then his arm reached out and snagged the lovely glass just before it hit the floor. "Better look at them on a stable surface," he said calmly, and set the bowl on the counter.

"Isn't it lovely?" She caught her breath at the beautiful object, vaguely aware that Caleb continued to trek up and down the stairs until boxes littered the floor of the small kitchen.

"You're still looking at that?" he said, huffing slightly as he set down the final box and closed the basement door. "Don't you want to see the rest?"

When Mia didn't immediately answer Caleb began removing more glass from the boxes. He lined them up across the counters. They were different shapes, color and sizes, some vases, some bowls, some functional, some simply to look at. And look Mia did. She also picked up several and examined their bases.

"You know what they are, don't you?" Caleb's gaze tracked her movements as she gently set down a flaming orange plate.

"I have an idea, but I'll have to check it out first." She wasn't quite ready to share her suspicions.

"They're certainly colorful. And I've figured out where they came from." Caleb grinned when she turned to look at him. "I think Harlan's mother was a collector. The label on three of the boxes is addressed to a Mrs. Granger."

"Really?" Mia bent, frowned, then rose. Feeling

his gaze on her, she walked to a shelf and pulled down a huge family Bible.

"What's wrong? Do you want me to leave?" he asked, clearly perplexed.

"No." She flipped open the heavy cover and slid her finger down the list of names until she came to the one she wanted. "Jane Granger."

"She was his mother?" He shrugged when she nodded. "There you have it, then."

"Do I?" Mia returned the Bible to the shelf and sank onto a chair. "Look at the name on those boxes, Caleb. Look closely." She held her breath as he squatted to get a better look. Then his head jerked. He stared at her over his shoulder.

"Mrs. M. Granger," he said very softly. "You."

"Me." Mia's brain felt swathed in cotton wool. She couldn't make sense of this. "Did Harlan buy them for me?"

"Then, why didn't he give them to you?" Caleb's voice hardened after he'd checked the labels again. "They're date stamped four years ago, received at his office."

"I don't understand this," Mia said helplessly. "I did a quilt design several years ago, which I loosely based on a glass artist named Lalique. I was trying to achieve his sense of movement and fluidity on fabric. I remember because it was the one time Harlan asked about my work." She gulped. "The timeline is right," she whispered to herself.

"So he realized you liked this artist, probably did his own research, found out the pieces were collectable and bought some for you." Caleb frowned. "But why not give them to you? Why not display them?"

"Here?" Mia tried to mask her scorn. "Hardly suitable. Not to mention the insurance he'd need."

"Then—" Caleb's silver gaze narrowed. "Riverbend?"

"I don't think so. It's not his type of place and there are no showcases." Mia fell silent as her brain drew the obvious conclusions. She couldn't quite believe Harlan would have done it to hurt her and yet... "He knew how much I loved Lalique and yet he left these beautiful things sitting down there with orders that I wasn't to touch them. To spite me?"

To spite me?

Caleb flinched at the hurt and confusion in Mia's words. He felt helpless as tears of sorrow trickled down her cheeks. How any man could be so callous of this sweet woman's feelings irritated him beyond measure, especially because Mia went out of her way to be kind and sensitive to everyone. He wanted to help her, to make it better, but what could he do? If he let her get too close, she'd realize he wasn't the man she thought. Then Mia would shed tears over him and the disappointment he'd caused her. The idea of being compared to her jerk of a husband made Caleb feel sick.

"I'm sorry." He touched her shoulder, trying to express his empathy.

"So am I." Mia lifted her chin, tears glittering on her lashes. "I'm sorry he felt he had to go behind my back. I wish my mother had never arranged our marriage. Harlan must have been so unhappy."

"*He* must have been unhappy?" Caleb couldn't stop the angry words. "How can you forgive him? He doesn't deserve your tears."

"Yes, he does." Mia wiped her cheeks and managed a tremulous smile before her gaze slid to admire the lovely glass. "All his secrets and lies must have made his life horrible."

"This Lalique—is it valuable?" Caleb asked mostly to get her to stop weeping over a man who'd never deserved her care and consideration.

"If they're authentic they may be worth a great deal." Mia brushed her hand against her wet eyelashes before summoning a smile. "You'd have to get them appraised."

"No, you would." He grinned. "And the books. They're yours, remember?"

Mia looked stunned. "I guess they are."

"Do you mind if I go through the main floor now? You need to tell me what changes you think should be made here and upstairs."

Caleb was surprised by Mia's acuity as she

pointed out areas of concern. Upstairs he gritted his teeth and forced himself not to comment on the shabby state of her room.

"It has to be freezing here in the winter," he said, noting the drafty window.

"It's not bad." Mia smiled. "I make quilts, remember?"

"Maybe you should start making rugs," he muttered to himself, and knew she'd heard by her throaty chuckle. What a good sport she was.

"This was Harlan's room." Mia stood at the doorway as if she was afraid to enter.

"Why don't you use this room?" Caleb asked, noting the expensive furnishings and thick carpet. "It feels much warmer."

"I couldn't do that." Her green eyes stretched wide. "It was his."

Distaste? Fear? Caleb couldn't decipher her expression, so he let it go and followed her to the bathroom.

"Total gut?" she asked.

He nodded, his silver eyes revealing his surprise. "Where did you—?"

"I heard it on TV," she said with a tiny smile. "I've always wanted to say it."

"Gutting this bathroom and simply leaving it that way would be an improvement." He realized immediately that he'd dissed her home and tried to make amends. "It's a lovely old house, though. The wood is superb. If this stairway was restored it would be magnificent. I'm glad you're going to bring her back to her former glory. I only wish you'd been able to live in it that way."

"Knowing someone else is enjoying the improvements will bring me a lot of joy." Mia led the way downstairs. Caleb thought she looked like a regal princess descending the palace staircase.

"You have someone in mind to live here, don't you?" When they reached the kitchen he saw the truth on her lovely face. "Someone special?"

"A wonderful man trying to raise two stepkids in a very trying situation. He's finding it tough to put a roof over their heads and feed them on his limited means." Mia's shy smile said everything he needed to know about this "friend." "I met him at church. His name is Arthur."

"Oh." Caleb pretended concentration as he wrote down the name of a contractor he trusted while trying to ignore the sprout of envy that had sprung to life inside his chest at the mention of this man with children. But how could he be jealous of a man he didn't even know?

Was he resentful because Mia was exactly the type to take on the mothering of two needy kids and do it superbly? Or was it because he feared this man and his children would diminish his chance of getting her to focus on mothering Lily?

It couldn't be for any personal reasons, because Caleb was not getting involved with Mia. His relationship with Lara had proved he was too jaded, too marked by his past to care for someone deeply enough to share his life with them. He was only here to help Mia as a friend.

So as a friend, he was officially worried about this Arthur, Caleb acknowledged privately. Maybe he'd stop by Mia's church on Sunday to vet the guy, make sure he wasn't pulling some kind of con job on her, as her husband had done.

But he was doing it because he was Mia's friend. And because of Lily.

Chapter Five

On the following Sunday, Caleb stood at the back of Mia's church searching for her distinctive strawberry blonde curls. Chagrined when he couldn't immediately spot her, he began to question his decision to bring Lily. He'd hoped to fuel the bond between her and Mia, but if she wasn't even here...

A tug on his hand drew Caleb's attention to Lily. She pointed to an empty pew three rows from the back. He nodded and followed her, smiling when the little girl lifted her pure clear voice to join in a hymn. He'd never known anyone who loved church as much as Lily. She'd only agreed to come with him to this one because she'd coaxed a promise of lunch from him.

Caleb's heart lurched into a gallop when he finally spotted Mia, who had moved forward and now waited at the front while kids' church was announced. Little ones from all over the congregation hurried toward her. Her lovely face glowed as she greeted each one with a bright smile. At Caleb's prompt Lily rose and limped toward Mia, too.

Mia's green eyes widened in surprise when she saw Lily. She held out a hand toward the child, then scanned the congregation until her gaze rested on Caleb. His pulse rate soared when her smile broadened. She turned her attention back to the children to shush them for the pastor's prayer. Then Mia and the children left.

Feeling better about his decision to come here, Caleb paused a moment to consider her obvious ease with the children. There had been no trace of fear on her face when she urged them from the sanctuary, but then he recalled the other workers who'd accompanied her. So it was only on her own that she became fearful? Puzzled and confused, he turned his attention to the bulletin and grimaced at the sermon title.

"When forgiveness is impossible."

Not again. Caleb consoled himself with the knowledge that at least here his father wasn't sitting behind him, watching and waiting. He'd brought Lily and Mia together again, but now he wished Lily had asked him to accompany her so he could avoid hearing the sermon.

"There is no sin too deep that God's forgiveness can't reach."

Caleb stiffened at the pastor's assertion.

"I said *no sin*. That includes everything you can think of and more besides." The short, bald-headed man chuckled. "God's seen it all, every ugly, dirty, shameful thing humans can do. And still He says we must forgive."

Caleb shifted uncomfortably, fuming that he'd chosen this Sunday to come to this church. Why hadn't he gone to his own church, and come to see Mia later?

"But forgiveness of something that's touched you personally isn't easy."

The words slammed into Caleb in spite of his intention to ignore that booming voice.

"When someone has wronged us, the hurt festers inside us. We grow less and less inclined to forgive."

Each word felt like a dart piercing him, yet Caleb couldn't shut them out.

When the pastor glanced over the congregation, Caleb felt as if his stare penetrated through the layers of bitterness and anger burning inside him and reached out to the kid inside him who still mourned his mother's death.

"What I am saying," the minister continued in a quieter tone, "is that we must get the spotlight off our poor miserable lives, let go of the unforgiving cancer that eats at us so we can become a healthy part of His family. That's when we will finally be free."

Was that how Mia seemed able to forgive her

husband's infidelity and cheating? Because she'd turned it over to God? Caleb longed to ignore the rest of the sermon, but the pastor's words kept him nailed to his seat, forcing Caleb to think deeply.

He was jerked from his thoughts when everyone rose to sing a hymn. While the pastor pronounced a benediction and dismissed the congregation, Caleb's brain churned with questions. How could God expect him to forgive the person who should have loved his wife, Caleb's mother, till death did them part?

Several people shook his hand and welcomed him before he saw Mia and Lily heading toward him. Mia's turquoise dress emphasized her lovely figure and glorious hair beautifully. Caleb smiled and pretended he wasn't staring.

"Lily is a very apt pupil." She brushed Lily's cheek tenderly. "It was a pleasure having her in our class."

"It was so fun, Uncle Caleb." Lily's dark blue eyes gleamed. "We went fishing just like Jesus's disciples did, only we didn't have real water."

"Cool." A pang stabbed through him to finally see she'd recaptured some of her joy. Lily was a lot like Mia; both of them found delight in the simplest things. "Did you catch anything?"

"Yes. And I ate it." She giggled.

"Only some fish-shaped crackers." Mia's gaze met his, then dropped. She seemed suddenly uncomfortable. "Well, I'd better go clean up."

"Can Mia come with us for lunch, Uncle Caleb? You promised you'd take me, remember?" Lily's dark blue eyes beseeched him to agree.

Funny how much he wanted to have lunch with Mia. Not seeing her this week felt as if he'd gone without coffee. The fulfillment he usually found in his work had been missing, too.

"Would you like to join us for lunch, Mia?" Caleb asked, expecting her to decline.

"I'd love to, if you're sure it's not an imposition," Mia said quietly. "I don't want to interfere with your time together."

"Me an' Uncle Caleb have lots of times together," Lily informed her. "He takes me for rides up in the hills sometimes."

"Takes you for rides?" Mia's curious gaze studied him.

"I ride in front of him, 'cause of my leg." Lily glanced down, then shrugged. "Me an' Uncle Caleb have a secret place where we go to watch the animals. We can see them, but they can't see us. We take snacks to eat and special glasses to watch them and sometimes we leave food for the animals. But not people food," she explained seriously.

"Of course not." Mia's glance drifted to him. "That's awfully nice of Uncle Caleb."

"Yeah. He's really nice. Don't you think?" Lily hugged his leg.

"I do," Mia agreed.

"Can we help you clean up?" Caleb asked to deflect their praise. She refused, but he and Lily followed her to the kids' center anyway. Some of the other workers had already straightened the room, so there wasn't much left to do but wash the plastic glasses the kids had used. Mia washed and Caleb dried while Lily played with a puppet.

"It's very kind of you to help." Mia's soft floral perfume reminded him of the Persian roses at Riverbend.

"How are things with you?" He found himself eager to catch up with her world.

"I got my driver's license." Her obvious delight in the accomplishment made him chuckle.

"Good for you. I guess the next step is to choose a vehicle. Or were you intending to use Harlan's car?" Caleb wished he hadn't asked when he saw her shudder.

"I'd prefer to sell that," Mia said in a flat tone.

"Then, do it." He frowned at her hesitation. "Why not?"

"I don't know. It seems so wasteful. I mean, I already own it and it works fine according to the garage." When her hand brushed his as she handed him the last glass, a tiny electric jolt speared through Caleb.

"So you sell someone a great car." Where once he might have felt irritation at her indecision, he now realized that each step Mia was taking on her own was a totally new experience. So he patiently waited as she mulled it over.

"I'd have to buy a new car." Mia drained and rinsed the sink. "Actually I'd like that, to have something all my own. But it's difficult because I have no idea how to choose. All I know is I'd like a red one." She winked at him. "Bright shiny red."

"Red's nice," he agreed, keeping his face solemn as he enjoyed her pleasure.

"But an impractical reason to choose a car." She frowned. "I've done lots of reading about vehicles, but now I'm more confused than before."

"Maybe you should test drive some and see how comfortable you feel in each," he said gently, sensing how overwhelmed she felt.

"Good idea," she applauded. "You always make everything sound so simple, logical."

"My dad Ben always says that if you can break your goal down into steps, you can take one step at a time and then it won't seem so overpowering." He hung up the tea towel on a nearby peg.

"A very sensible man, your dad." Mia's smile coaxed Caleb to agree.

Just then Lily walked over and folded her hand in his.

"What's wrong?" He hunkered down so she could whisper in case she didn't want Mia to hear. But Lily didn't whisper.

"I'm so hungry my stomach is eating my back, Uncle Caleb."

He shouted with laughter, knowing exactly where that saying came from. "You're copying Grandpa Ben now, aren't you?"

"Yes." She tilted her dark head to one side. "But it's true."

"Then we'd better go eat something. Hamburgers?" She shook her head. "Hot dogs?" Same reaction. Caleb hid his smile. "Pizza, then."

"Uncle Caleb, you promised we could have waffles." Lily frowned.

"Yes, I did." He tapped the end of her nose with his forefinger. "And I always keep my promises. Waffles it is. Okay, Mia?"

"Perfect." Mia picked up her purse and a matching jacket. "I love waffles."

"With strawberries?" Lily asked.

"Or blueberries," Mia agreed. "And whipped cream and maybe some bacon." She turned to Caleb. "I'll pay for half."

He almost laughed until he realized she was perfectly serious. So he simply said, "This is my treat, Mia. I promised Lily."

"Okay. But next time it's my turn." She accepted Lily's hand in hers and the three of them left the church, neither female aware of just how much Caleb wanted there to be a next time.

He drove to the restaurant, letting Lily chat with Mia while he noted every car dealership along the way. It would be an easy matter to stop after lunch to admire his favorite vehicle. Then they could "happen" to test-drive the vehicles in which Mia showed interest.

But Caleb's subterfuge wasn't necessary because after lunch Mia asked him if he'd mind taking her to look at a small SUV she'd admired online. While she spoke with the salesman he did a quick search on his phone. The vehicle was rated highly, had no known major defects and came in the bright Christmas red Mia yearned for.

"What do you think?" she asked him a few minutes later.

"I think you should test-drive it. If it doesn't fit you, you don't want it." Caleb wanted Mia to experience choosing her own car based on her own feelings, hoping it would help her find confidence in her decisions.

When the salesman returned with the keys, he and Mia walked with Lily to the red car. Caleb had to hide his amusement at Mia's worried look as she sat behind the wheel.

"You're a licensed driver now," he murmured in her ear through the open window. "You can handle whatever challenges you meet."

Mia's shoulders went back, she sat a little taller in the seat and her grip on the wheel loosened. After a moment she met his gaze.

"Thank you. I think you're the nicest man I've ever met, Caleb Grant." After tossing him a quick smile she started the car and drove away, leaving him staring after her.

The nicest man? Guilt rushed in. He was trying to get Mia to care for Lily so she'd take over as Lily's benefactor. Was that being nice?

"What are we going to do now, Uncle Caleb?" Lily asked.

"We're going to sit in my car and wait for Mia to come back." He waited till she was settled, then climbed in beside her. "You like Mia, don't you?"

"Uh-huh. She doesn't cluck with her teeth when she looks at my leg," Lily said.

Her words made Caleb do a double take.

"Do lots of people do that?" he asked curiously.

"Uh-huh. Then they look away and say, 'Poor thing.'" She tilted her head and frowned at him. "Am I poor, Uncle Caleb?"

He shook his head immediately and reached over to hug her. "You're not poor, Lily, because your heart is rich with love."

"Oh." She gave him a dubious look. "I don't know e'zackly what that means."

"It means I think you're the best kid in the whole world," he said, and brushed a kiss against the top of her head.

"I love you, too, Uncle Caleb." Lily flung her arms around his neck and hugged him. "I wish you could 'dopt, me but Ms. Vermeer says you won't," she mumbled into his shirtfront. "How come?"

"Well, I can't adopt you, Lily, because I wouldn't be a good daddy. I don't know how." Caleb squeezed the words out around the lump in his throat. He wasn't sure where this overwhelming need to protect Lily had come from. He only knew that he was her godfather, and her godmother, Lara, would have wanted, no, expected him to watch out for her niece.

"I could show you how to be a daddy, Uncle Caleb." Lily's earnest tone nearly undid him.

"I would like that more than anything, sweetheart. But it just can't be." He held her as a rush of sadness filled him. This was why he couldn't forgive his father, because Joel had ruined Caleb's ability to love and care for anyone.

"Is it 'cause you don't have a house?" Lily wiggled free. "Grandma Marsha told Ms. Vermeer you're gonna sell Auntie Lara's ranch."

"I have to, honey," he admitted. "Because I don't know how to love the animals like your aunt did." *I don't know how to love anyone.*

"Oh." Lily sighed. "I'm like Auntie Lara's animals. I don't have a home, either."

"I will find you a home, Lily," he promised for what felt like the hundredth time. "But you have to be patient."

"And I hafta pray. That's what Mia told me." Lily grinned at him. "She said I got to tell God what I want and wait for Him to answer."

"That's good advice." Caleb's heart pinched for this child's sweet heart and for Mia's gentle soul.

Maybe if he tried harder he could make her see that she'd be a great mom for Lily.

"I sure hope my mom is happy. Do you think she is, Uncle Caleb?" Lily's sad voice broke through his introspection.

Caleb gulped and searched for the right answer. But he couldn't find one. All he could think of to say was "I'm sure she didn't like leaving you alone, Lily. She loved you very much."

"I know." Lily sighed and laid her head back against her seat. A moment later one fat tear tumbled down her cheek. "Mia said my mom's with God, but I wish she was with me."

Caleb felt useless and helpless as Lily gave way to sobs. He cradled her in his arms, knowing it was only natural for the little girl to miss her mother, but still feeling he should be able to do something to ease her loss. Something more than sitting here, letting her cry.

Was it wrong to feel a surge of relief when Mia came driving back onto the lot?

Sensing something had happened between Caleb and Lily, Mia made an excuse to the salesman and hurried back to the pair in the car. Caleb drove her home without saying a word. Lily was also quiet.

"Will you come in for a few minutes?" she invited. "The house is a mess, but I can offer coffee and juice."

"You've started the renovation already?" Caleb's eyes widened. "I'd like to see it."

"Come in, then." She led them inside hesitantly, wondering if Caleb would approve of the changes she'd asked for. As she feared, his face was tight with disapproval when he finished surveying the main floor. "You don't like it."

"It's going to look amazing, but, Mia, you can't live here during this." He waved a hand at the broken drywall, the half-removed walls and the debris scattered everywhere. "It's a mess."

"I'm managing," she said defensively.

"But you shouldn't have to manage. I should have thought of this earlier," he said, his anger obvious. "I know. Why don't you move into Riverbend and save yourself this aggravation?"

"I wish I could." She dug out a glass for Lily and poured some juice into it. "Here are some cookies, too," she offered, clearing a space at the table for the little girl. Then she started the coffeemaker. "There's some problem with taking possession of Riverbend. Bella said there's a lien on it for unpaid taxes."

"Harlan didn't pay them?" Caleb's confused look mirrored her thoughts.

"Apparently not. I instructed Bella to do that so they're now up-to-date," Mia explained. "But the municipality is demanding what Bella feels is an excessive amount of interest. She's trying to sort it out."

"Well, she needs to hurry because clearly you can't keep living here." His glance held irritation. "Where do you work?"

"In the sunroom."

"But there's no heat! And it's been below freezing the past couple of days." Caleb's lips pinched in a tight line. "I'm going to call Mayor Marsha and see if she can help."

"Your mother?" Confused, Mia watched him pull out his phone. "What can she do? She's mayor of Buffalo Gap, not the municipality."

"She has some sway because Buffalo Gap helped the municipality out a few years ago. Maybe they'll listen to her and expedite the situation." He began speaking into his phone. Mia turned away and chatted with Lily, glimpsing her home through Caleb's critical eyes.

It was a mess. Maybe she shouldn't have brought them in here. But she'd been so proud of the changes in this shabby old house. Even in such disrepair it seemed full of promise.

"Okay, get your things together, Mia." Caleb shoved his phone into his pocket, then held out his hand to accept the coffee she'd poured.

"What do you mean?" she asked in confusion.

"You're leaving here. Mom texted Abby and she says there's room at Family Ties. You can stay there until Bella can get you into Riverbend." He finally noticed her shaking head and moderated his voice. "It's safe there, Mia. You'll have a quiet place to work and you can use the kitchen to cook whatever you need, or you can eat out."

"But—" She gaped at him, unable to imagine walking away from this mess. "I can't just leave my home!"

"Why not?" After a second survey of the room, Caleb shrugged. "You've already moved out most of the furniture. I'm sure the workers would find it much easier to do their jobs with you out of here, too. They wouldn't have to worry about disturbing you or making a mess and you wouldn't have to shiver in that fridge of a workroom. It's the perfect solution."

A warm area to work did sound good, Mia admitted privately. And time to think without constant hammering. Then, too, there was Buffalo Gap's gorgeous landscape to consider. It would be her inspiration for a new project.

"But how will I get around?" she asked. "I doubt there are city buses in Buffalo Gap."

"That is a problem." Caleb thought for a moment. "Maybe you could drive Harlan's car for a day or two, just till you're settled. Then you could sell it and buy what you really want."

Mia suppressed her shudder. She didn't want to even sit in Harlan's car, let alone drive it, but it was a solution she was loath to ignore. Besides, the thought of escaping this mess now excited her.

"What about the women at Family Ties? Will they mind me moving in?" she asked.

"I doubt they'll even notice you're there. Family Ties was once a hotel. It's been renovated, but it's still huge with lots of room. Abby told Mom they're running at less than one-third full, so you're more than welcome. You'll love Abby." Caleb looked supremely confident.

"How can you be sure?" Mia asked curiously.

"Because Abby is exactly like you. Big, generous heart trying to help every needy person who crosses her path." His grin made him look younger. "You could be sisters."

"But I've never even met her. I don't like to just show up," Mia protested. But Caleb had an answer for that, too.

"Call her." He dialed a number, spoke to someone then held out the phone. "Go ahead. You'll see that Abby Lebret has the same soft heart as you."

Ten minutes later, reassured by Abby's warm welcome, Mia sat in the driver's seat of Harlan's car, now packed full of her things, and followed Caleb to Buffalo Gap.

"Lord," she prayed as she drove, "I trust You to direct my path so I'm moving temporarily to Family Ties. Please help me be a light for You. And please help me find a way to help Caleb. After all, he's done a lot for me." A little glow of warmth puddled inside her.

She really liked Caleb. Maybe too much?

Chapter Six

On Friday, a week later, Caleb walked down Main Street on his way to pick up Mia at Family Ties. Crowds attending Buffalo Gap's Harvest Days filled the streets for the annual event in mid-October. Since local retailers stayed open extended hours to run deeply discounted sidewalk sales, hurrying through the throngs of eager shoppers was difficult.

About to cross the street, Caleb stopped in his tracks. Joel Crane, his biological father was heading straight for him. Immediately Caleb's hackles went up, but with half the town mingling around them he refused to make a scene. He despised the gossip and innuendo he'd overheard since his father's arrival, but he wasn't about to back down or run away now, so he stood his ground and waited.

"Caleb." A tentative smile flickered across his father's face. "I was hoping to talk to you."

"I have nothing to say to you." Guilt chewed at

his insides when a hurt-puppy-dog look washed across Joel's face.

"But *I* have something to say to *you*, and it's important. Please listen." Joel touched his arm, but Caleb shook off his hand. "I didn't kill her, son. I loved your mother. I wouldn't have hurt her for anything in this world."

"Wouldn't you?" Infuriated, Caleb demanded, "You don't think it hurt her when her husband came home drunk, called her names and bullied her when he didn't get his way? We don't have anything to discuss," he grated. "Stay away from me."

While his father protested, Caleb sidestepped him and continued toward Family Ties, seething.

"Caleb?"

A hand on his arm made him flinch. He whirled around. Mia stood behind him.

"You walked right past me," she said.

"Sorry." He exhaled heavily. "I just had a run-in with my father. You might want to reschedule our lunch. I'm not in a very good mood."

"Why don't we walk for a bit? I've been painting and I need some exercise." She looped her arm through his and tugged on it to get him to move. "Isn't it a gorgeous day? It seems like winter's eons away."

"Don't kid yourself. We often have snow in early October. This year we've been lucky." The mundane subject and Mia's bright cheery tone chased away his dark mood. "What have you been painting? No, don't tell me. Scenery."

"Yes." Her smile caused a flush of heat to warm Caleb's frozen heart. "But not only that. Family Ties is wonderful, full of stories. Abby's amazing. So are the two young women in residence. Their resilience is inspiring. One of them, Jan, is working on a little garden area at the back of the building."

"Fall bulbs, I suppose." Caleb frowned. "But she won't be here to see them bloom."

"Preparing the area makes Jan's heart bloom now." Mia's kindly voice soothed. "Someone else will benefit from her work in the spring."

"If it helps her I'm glad. I've been working with both of those women. Giving up a child isn't easy and Jan in particular feels very guilty. It's even more important to make sure her child has a wonderful home." When Mia moved toward the town park, Caleb matched her steps, noting how the tension had left him. Funny how when he was around Mia his day always seemed brighter.

"You really care about your clients. I like that. What did your father want?"

The unexpected question brought back Caleb's tension. He struggled to suppress his negative feelings but Mia noticed. She stopped beside a park bench, sat down and patted the spot next to her.

"Talk to me, Caleb," she invited in that sensitive way she had.

"I don't—" He stopped, surprised when her eyebrows drew together in a severe line.

"I think we can safely say that you've listened to my problems more than anyone should have to," she said in a firm tone. "It's about time I repaid the favor, so talk."

"There's not much to say. He's looking for forgiveness. I can't offer that." Caleb added, "I doubt I ever will."

"Okay, but couldn't you at least listen to him? You're his son. He misses you, wants to reconnect. You don't have to offer anything," she said when he glared at her. "But you could listen."

"No." Caleb shook his head. "I can't."

"Because?"

"Because he doesn't deserve it." He stiffened when she chuckled. "That's funny?"

"Yes, it's very funny." Mia patted his hand as if to apologize, but her next words astonished him. "None of us deserve anything, Caleb. People say, 'I deserve this,' but we don't *deserve* anything. Thankfully God loves us in spite of our unworthiness."

"That's not right." He stared, confounded by her logic.

"Yes, it is." Mia lifted her face into the sunshine. "God forgives us, not because we deserve it, but because He loves us. So, to me, it seems wrong when we who have been forgiven with such grace won't forgive others."

"So you've forgiven Harlan for deceiving you?" he shot back, and hated himself for saying it when a cloud dimmed the light in her lovely eyes.

"I'm trying." She gave him a reproachful look. "It isn't easy, but I'm trying to remember that he didn't understand love. He was afraid of it. I can't hate him for being afraid."

"I don't think that's a good enough excuse for what he did." Before Caleb could say more, Mia jumped to her feet.

"It's my reason. Can we eat now?" Her loveliness made him catch his breath as she danced from one foot to the other, waiting for him. "I'm starving. And this time I am buying, so no arguments. Got it?"

"Yes, ma'am." Her severe tone couldn't suppress her resurfacing smile, and that amused him. "Where are you taking me?"

"That place over there." She pointed to Eats, the priciest place in town. "Abby said they have the best lasagna, and that is exactly what I've been craving. Make sure you eat enough because you're going to need it."

"I am?" Caleb thought he'd never known anyone who found such sheer delight in life. Mia was embracing everything that came her way and somehow turned it into joy. "Why?"

"Because, Caleb, tomorrow morning I'm moving into Riverbend Ranch, and I'm hoping you'll help me." Ecstatic, Mia grabbed his hands and swung in a circle around him. Her happiness spilled all over him, chasing away the shadows of the past.

"At last. Congratulations," he said. "Of course I'll help." Caught up in the joy of her news, Caleb grasped her waist, lifted her and swung her round, thrilling at her peal of laughter.

Mia's elation and hope was contagious, but suddenly her eyes met his and Caleb realized how intimate the moment had become. Slowly he lowered her to the ground and gently released her, reluctant to let go of this amazing joy-filled woman but knowing he couldn't allow her to burrow into his heart. Because he couldn't bear to see hurt fill her expressive eyes when she realized he had nothing to offer her.

Mia balanced awkwardly for a moment, but before he could reach out an arm for support she righted herself. Her eyes held his, probing, asking questions, waiting.

"I hope you'll be very happy at Riverbend, Mia," he said sincerely.

"I will be. It's going to be my new start," she said in a firm tone. "I'm going to have a wonderful life."

"You deserve it." The words slipped out before he realized it. He glanced at her, saw her lips twitch and couldn't stop his own chuckle. "Well, you do."

"No, I don't. But I thank God He's given it to me. And I don't want to argue with you, so let's go eat." She grabbed his hand once more.

Caleb followed, content to escape the intimacy of the previous moments but reveling in the pleasure of her company. He liked Mia, liked her spunk, her plucky courage, her determination to find a bright spot in everything. But there could never be more than friendship between them because, although he was certain that Mia was full of love just waiting to be poured out, he was not.

"I suppose you have to get back to the office soon." When Caleb forgot about his father, he was utterly charming. Mia hated to see their time together end.

"Not necessarily." He leaned back in his chair. "Did you have something in mind?"

"No. I'm just enjoying relaxing with you. Hearing about your childhood on the Grants' ranch is interesting." She waited until their server had brought his chocolate cake and he'd tasted it. "I've never been around animals much. I don't think my mother liked the mess they caused. She loved order."

"As a kid I had lots of pets." He grinned at the memories. "A pet raven, a bull. Once I even had a pet snake, though that ended when Marsha found its hiding place. She is deathly afraid of them."

"Me, too." Mia couldn't suppress her chuckle. When Caleb arched one dark eyebrow to ask why, she tapped the side of her cheek. "You look very nice in chocolate icing," she teased, "but not very lawyerly."

He made a face as he dabbed his napkin to remove the spot. "Want a taste?" he asked, holding out his fork loaded with icing.

"No, thanks." She shuddered. "That's enough sugar to add ten pounds."

"With your energy level?" Caleb continued eating, but she knew his brain was dwelling on something else.

"I don't eat a lot of sugar. Harlan's mother died from diabetes and it was something he was always warning me about." Caleb didn't need to know how often she'd eaten sweets in private to avoid those comments.

"You won't hear me putting down this good stuff," Caleb promised, savoring his cake with obvious enjoyment.

"I want to ask you a nosy question, but you may not want to answer it," Mia said, deciding to broach a subject that had been bothering her for a while. Though his eyes narrowed, he didn't immediately shut her down. She liked that.

"You can ask," he invited in that rumbly voice she found so attractive.

"You clearly love Lily. Why don't you adopt her?" She hadn't finished the question before Caleb began shaking his head.

"I can't," he said, his voice bleak.

"Because?" she pressed. Did the flickering in his silver-gray eyes mean he was hiding something from her?

"Well, for starters, I don't have a home anymore." He pushed away the rest of his uneaten cake. "I received an offer on the ranch this morning. I'm accepting it."

"Congratulations." His lack of expression piqued her curiosity. "That's good news, isn't it?"

"Yes and no." He shrugged. "They want possession before winter, so I need to move out fairly soon."

"You must have thought about somewhere else to live in Buffalo Gap when you listed it." Mia tried not to be too obvious in studying his reactions, but she was intrigued by his blunt refusal to consider adoption.

"I've looked at a few places, but I don't want to make any quick decisions. That's kind of what I did when Lara and I bought the ranch," he admitted.

"And you were sorry?" Were those shadows in his eyes regret?

"If Lara had lived, it would have been perfect. I could have helped her achieve her dream. But I never even considered I'd be left to run it. I've failed so miserably I had to have someone take all the animals."

"I'm sure you did your best. I doubt Lara would ask more than that," Mia soothed. "So now you have nowhere to live and that's why you can't adopt Lily?"

"Actually I do have a place to live. My parents have a little cabin on their land, beside the river." A funny little smile twisted Caleb's lips. "Dad used to be an outfitter. Over the years they've had hunters, birdwatchers, fishermen stay there in all seasons. It's a bit primitive and certainly no place for Lily, but I can make do."

"Is that what you want?" There was something in his words she didn't quite understand. Reluctance, perhaps? "To make do?"

"No. I want my own place, a ranch but without cattle. A place with lots of space and freedom." The words died away, as if he didn't want to give away too much.

"So at heart you are a cowboy," she teased.

"Always," he said with a chuckle.

"But it won't have a place for Lily." Immediately his face tightened and Mia knew she'd pushed too hard.

"Look, I'm not the person to raise Lily," he said, lips tightening with his irritation. "She's a great kid, but it would be wrong for me to even try to be her father."

"Wrong?" Mia didn't want to keep pushing, but

in her mind Caleb would be the perfect father. "Is it her leg?"

"Her leg?" His eyes widened and then narrowed. "The fact that Lily has a damaged leg has nothing to do with it. It's because of me, because I can't be who she needs. Can we leave now?"

"I'm keeping you from work. I'm sorry." Mia waved to their server and handed him her brand-new credit card. While they waited, she gathered her things, aware of the tension between them. She signed the receipt, added a generous tip and rose.

"Thank you for lunch," Caleb said, sounding slightly mollified.

"Thank you for joining me." Mia walked out of the restaurant and waited until they were walking across the park, some distance from the restaurant before she let out a little whoop. "That felt so good." She grinned, delighted with herself.

"What did?" The mystified look on his face made her burst out laughing.

"Paying for lunch. Independence," she explained. "I've never had a credit card before. Harlan liked to live on cash."

"Harlan liked to have you locked up, without access to any assets," Caleb corrected sourly. "Never mind that they are *your* assets."

"Let it go, Caleb." She held his gaze. "It's the past. It doesn't matter now. I'm moving into a new home of my own. I don't want to tarnish that with ugly thoughts. Be happy for me?" she begged, touching his arm with her fingertips. "Please?"

He studied her for several wordless moments. Finally his fingers curled around hers, warm and comforting. "Of course I'm happy for you, Mia. I can't think of anyone who deserves a new home more." He smiled, squeezed her hand, then let it go. "Though I still can't help wondering why he bought Riverbend."

"Maybe someday we'll know. I believe God had a hand in it. Oh, look. It's Lily." Mia's heart squeezed tight at the sight of the little girl sitting on a swing in the park's playground, head down, shoulders dropping in a dejected way. "Why is she alone?"

"Hilda's place is right over there. Look, she's sitting on the front porch watching." Caleb lifted a hand and waved. Hilda waved back.

"Lily looks so sad. Let's go cheer her up." Mia started toward the little girl, glad that Caleb followed without question.

"Hi, Lily," she murmured, kneeling by the child. "How are you?"

"Sad." Lily looked up, face streaked with tears. "I'm an orphan."

Behind her, Mia heard Caleb groan.

"Who told you that, honey?" She brushed dark wet strands of hair away from the child's tearstained cheeks.

"Some kids at school. They said orphans get

sent to houses where they have to work for their food." Lily sniffed. "My leg hurts sometimes. Maybe I can't work hard enough. I get awful hungry."

"Sweetheart, you're never going to have to work for your food." Caleb hunkered down beside Mia, his voice warm and tender with reassurance. "I'm going to make sure you're always cared for. And you're not an orphan."

"How come?" Lily frowned at him, her gaze questioning. "My teacher read us a story about orphans. An orphan is a child who doesn't got a family. That's me."

"But you do have a family, darlin'." The tenderness of Caleb's voice sent a rush of sweetness through Mia's heart. What a good man he was. Her heart pinched when he slid an arm around Lily's tiny waist, lifted her from the swing and hugged her against his side. "You have a family who cares about you very much."

"Who?" Lily's voice wobbled, as if she was afraid to believe what he was saying.

"Well, you've got me. *Uncle* Caleb, remember? Uncles are family." He tickled her under the chin. "And you've got Mia. And you've got Ms. Vermeer looking after you, and Grandma Marsha and Grandpa Ben. They're all your family and they love you very much."

"We all care about you, Lily. We love you very

much," Mia added, struggling to keep her voice from breaking. "You're not alone."

"But that's not real family." Lily sniffed. "A real family has a mommy and a daddy."

"Listen to me, darlin'." Caleb tipped her chin so she had to look at him. "What makes a family isn't a mommy or a daddy. What makes a family is love." His fingertip smoothed away her tears. His voice oozed compassion and caring. "You are loved so much, my sweet Lily."

Mia wanted to weep at the tenderness of his words and the love glowing in his silver eyes. As Lily's smile peeked out she longed to wrap her arms around both of them and hang on. This big tenderhearted man had put aside his own inhibitions about love to reassure a little lost girl. Caleb would make a wonderful father. If only she could convince him to adopt Lily.

"Why didn't Hilda come with you to the park?" Caleb said when several minutes had passed.

"'Cause I yelled at her an' told her not to. I ran away." An ashamed look turned Lily's face sultry. "I was mad at those kids."

"Hilda cares about you a lot, Lily. See, she's sitting over there all alone." Caleb brushed a tender hand over the little girl's head. "She must be very worried to see you so upset. You need to apologize."

"I know." Lily's head hung with shame.

"I'll go with you." Caleb rose, clasping her

tiny hand in his. His eyes met Mia's. "Will you come, too?"

"I'd love to." Mia walked with the somber pair back to Ms. Hilda's, where Lily offered her apology and was quickly tearfully embraced.

"You sure are a lucky girl." Mia watched her as they munched on Hilda's fresh cookies. "A lot of people care about you."

"I know." Lily looked down. "I didn't mean to be bad. I just wanted my mommy back so I could be a family." A lonely tear clung to her eyelashes.

Mia couldn't just sit there and not do something. Caleb was there. Surely nothing bad could happen with him watching, nothing like what had happened before. She wrapped her arm around the little girl and snuggled her against her side.

"Tell me about your mom, Lily."

Lily talked for a while about the things she remembered best. Then she drank her milk and ate her last cookie before asking, "Will you tell me about your mommy, Mia?"

Mia glanced around. Caleb had returned to his office for a meeting, but Ms. Hilda was sitting a few feet away on her porch knitting. She wasn't alone with Lily.

"Please?" Lily begged.

"My mom was a lawyer, kind of like your uncle Caleb," Mia began. "Her job was to help people and she worked very hard to do that."

"What about your daddy?" Lily asked.

"I didn't have one. I asked my mother about him once," Mia murmured, suddenly transplanted back in time to her tenth birthday. "My mom got a very sad look on her face and said he'd gone away and wasn't going to come back. I could see that talking about him made her sad, so I never asked about him again."

"That's like my daddy!" Lily sat up straight, eyes flashing. "When I was little I asked my mom who my daddy was. She said I didn't have one. That night I heard her crying, so I didn't ask about my daddy anymore."

"It's hard to understand grown-ups sometimes, isn't it?" Mia comforted. "But we all have a daddy, one who loves us very much."

"You mean God, don't you, Mia?" Lily nodded. "Auntie Lara talked about Him all the time. My mommy was her sister. Auntie Lara said her and mommy's daddy was God and He was the best-est dad anyone could have."

"Auntie Lara was right," Mia said, thankful for Lara's faith. "God loves us very much. We can talk to Him whenever we want. He doesn't get tired or go away or get too busy to listen. He's always with us."

"I know." Lily snuggled against her side. "God's a nice daddy, isn't He, Mia? I think He's kind of like Caleb. I love Caleb."

"He loves you, too, sweetheart." Mia reveled in

the joy of having the sweet girl tucked against her side as the autumn sun warmed them.

Oh, God, I want a family, too, she prayed silently. *I want a child just like Mia. Please, could You erase the past and make it possible for me to be a mother? Please?*

But even as she prayed, she knew it couldn't be. She'd hurt an innocent child. Unwittingly, true, but that child had died because of her. She couldn't be trusted with another. So the next best thing was to get Caleb Grant to see that he was the perfect father for Lily.

"I think I've worn you out already." Mia chuckled when Caleb blinked his eyes open and pushed away from the kitchen island. "I thought Saturday would be your best day. That's why I chose today to move."

"Huh?" He frowned.

"Because it's your day off," she clarified. "Like you'd have more energy? I guess I should have found more moving helpers for my move to Riverbend."

"You should have bought less stuff," he shot back, enjoying the happy smile she'd been wearing all day. "I'm just thankful that furniture stores deliver. Carrying in all your quilt fabric has aged me ten years, though."

"Poor old man. We're almost finished." She

held out a tray of doughnuts. "Have another to give you some energy."

"No, thanks. I'm already on a sugar high." He glanced around the kitchen, a little shocked by how quickly she'd made it look like home. Shiny new copper pots swung from a rack above the massive stove. Bright green accents scattered here and there made it look as if Mia had cooked in this kitchen for years. The whole effect was enhanced by strategic placing of vigorous plants he'd helped her unload from her car. "Are you satisfied with it?"

"Mmm, pretty close," she mused. "Let's take a tour and I'll make notes of what else I need. Starting with my workroom."

"Do I have to go in there again?" he teased. "Your talent scares me a little."

"How?" She turned on him in surprise.

"You do everything so well. It's intimidating." He looked around the room. Her bright paintings hung everywhere, bringing light and happiness. "I think you need another lamp in here for nighttime."

"I have another, but I can't remember where it is." She sounded as if she was concentrating on something else. He'd learned that look in her eyes meant she'd begun visualizing another design for her quilt fabric. "The built-ins are perfect for storing my fabric." She hugged herself. "I'm going to love working here."

"Let's look at the rest." He left and walked to the living room, pushing away the urge to replace her arms with his. "I thought this room was too big, but your interior designer was right. The huge furniture makes it cozy, along with the fire." He sank into the plump cushions with a sigh. "I still think you should have chosen leather, but…"

"Leather's too cold. I've had enough cold to last me a lifetime." Mia inclined her head toward the dining room. "It looks great but it's intimidating. I don't know enough people to fill all those chairs."

"You soon will." Caleb grinned at her frown but didn't pursue the matter. "Upstairs?"

She nodded and preceded him up the winding staircase. "This is my room," she said as she pushed open the double doors.

"It's lovely." Which was an understatement, Caleb decided. Among the azure blues and deep sea greens Mia radiated like a mermaid in her ocean. "I thought maybe you'd choose white and frilly," he mumbled, not intending for her to hear.

Mia laughed. "Frilly? Not my style."

"But this isn't the master bedroom," Caleb exclaimed.

"That's too big for just me." Her cheeks turned an attractive pink. "Besides, I like this view of the garden better." As she led the way down the hall, he saw her glance below to the courtyard at the front of the house. "There are a whole lot of cars arriving," she said in a surprised tone.

"Uh-huh." Caleb grinned at her. "They're here for you, for a housewarming."

"For me?" Mia stared at him. "They don't even know me."

"That's why they're here," he said with a chuckle. "Do you think we should go and greet them?"

"Oh. Yes, of course." Mia led the way downstairs. "I wish I'd had time to change into something less casual."

"You look great. They'll love you. Stop worrying," Caleb said.

"How did they know I was moving in today?" she asked.

"I told them." He grinned, then reached around her to fling the door wide.

Caleb knew Mia's head was whirling as people flowed into her new home bearing dishes of savory goodness and gifts they insisted were simply a welcome to the community.

"We want you to feel at home and free to call on any of us at any time," Mayor Marsha said, speaking for the group. "Everyone's a neighbor in Buffalo Gap." Her gaze moved from the open door to Caleb. *"Everyone,"* she said pointedly.

Not understanding her emphasis on that word, Caleb glanced out the door and saw Joel standing there.

"Why, Mother?" Caleb demanded in a low voice.

"He's a part of our community now, Caleb," she

said in a firm tone. "We've never excluded or ostracized anyone and we're not going to start with your biological father."

Acutely aware of the many sets of curious eyes around him, Caleb debated walking out the door, until he glanced at Mia. She'd been so happy moments before. He couldn't ruin this for her, but he wasn't going to talk to Joel Crane either. Not today. Not ever. He stalked away.

The small, older man who watched Caleb walk away with hope dying was the man who'd murdered Caleb's mother? Mia's heart ached for the two as Caleb left and his father's shoulders slumped at the snub. The entire room had fallen silent. She stepped forward.

"Please come in," she invited, holding out her hand. "I'm Mia Granger."

"Thank you," he said so quietly she barely heard him. "I'm Joel Crane. Caleb's—" His chin drooped.

"Father," she finished loud enough for the others to hear. "Welcome here. Thank you for coming."

Marsha began directing operations, and the awkwardness of the moment dissipated as Mia's guests resumed chatting with each other.

"It isn't much but I brought some chips and dip," Joel said. "I'm afraid I'm not a very good cook."

"Among other things." Caleb now stood at her elbow, his glare fierce.

"Caleb, please," she whispered, standing on tip-toe to whisper in his ear. "This is my first real home. I want to enjoy it, for people to feel welcome here. Please don't spoil this for me." Mia slid her arm in his, knowing how deep his aversion for his biological father went and yet desperate to keep the peace. "Please?"

The ice in his silver eyes made her insides quiver. A moment later her heart sank as he nodded and then excused himself.

"I'll go," Joel said, and handed her the bag of chips. "Marsha insisted I come, but she was wrong. I don't belong here."

"You live in Buffalo Gap, don't you?" Mia asked. At his nod she smiled and threaded an arm through his. "Then, you belong here. Let's meet these people."

Actually her guests introduced themselves to her, none of them showing the least bit of anger or judgment that Joel Crane was among them. Except for Caleb. He hung in the background, watching everything with his icy glare. Mia was on her way to talk to him when a shout stopped her.

"Mia!" Lily hobbled across the room and threw herself into Mia's arms. "I came to see your new house."

"I'm glad you did." She hugged the little girl tightly, then glanced at her other guest. "Welcome, Ms. Hilda. Is that some of your delicious lemon pie?"

Hilda said that it was, then hurried toward the kitchen. That was when Mia heard Lily say, "You're Caleb's dad." Her head tilted to one side when Joel nodded. "He's mad at you," she said.

"Honey, Joel and I are meeting people. Would you like to come along?" Mia intervened.

"Uh-uh. I want to talk to Uncle Caleb about my birthday party." Lily awkwardly hurried away.

"I have apologized to Caleb for causing the accident with his mother, you know," Joel murmured. "Or tried to. He won't hear me."

"I know," Mia whispered, and squeezed his hand. "Caleb is in a lot of pain. We'll just have to keep praying that God will touch his heart."

"That's why I've stayed here," Joel admitted. "I keep praying God will heal the breach between my son and me. Meanwhile I accept whatever jobs I can get and wait."

"I'll pray, too," she promised.

They finished their tour of the room. At the end of it, Mia was certain she'd never remember all the names. Then Mayor Marsha said a short grace and announced that there was enough food for everyone to help themselves. Mia stood in a corner, content to watch and listen, savoring the pleasure of having her friends and neighbors share food in her home.

For the first time in ages she didn't feel left

out or on the sidelines. Today she felt as though she had taken the first step to truly belonging. Thanks to Caleb.

"Are you angry at me?" Caleb's quiet voice broke her introspection.

"For what? This?" She waved a hand toward the crowd. "This makes me extremely happy. It's exactly how I wanted Riverbend Ranch to be. Full of friends, fun and happiness. It's an answer to my prayers." She blushed as she said the words that lay on her heart. "You are an answer to prayer, Caleb. I'll never be able to thank you enough for helping me take this step."

"You did it on your own," he said before accepting a cupcake from a tray Abby Lebret was passing around. "But as long as you don't mind me inviting half the town…"

"I'm glad you did," she said. "You're the best friend I ever had."

Best friend?

Caleb smothered his frown. Nothing worse than being a best friend to a lovely woman. Especially one as beautiful as Mia.

"I've never had many friends." Mia's gaze followed Lily as she limped from one person to the next, her eyes dancing with excitement as she chatted. "Not like Lily has. Everyone seems to love her."

"What about the friend from church who's

going to live in your other house?" Caleb hoped he didn't sound as disgruntled by the knowledge as he felt.

"You mean Arthur?" Mia blinked at him looking startled. "I guess I never thought of him like that."

"He's *not* a friend, but you're letting him live in your house?" Caleb said.

"Yes, because of his grandchildren." Mia's green eyes darkened. "Their mother's in rehab. Their father abandoned them. Their grandfather is trying to put some stability in their lives. I thought living in the house instead of their tiny apartment could help him do that."

Caleb couldn't speak because of a coughing fit caused by choking on his cupcake. He'd spent all this time being jealous of a *grandfather*? And why was he jealous anyway? Mia was nothing to him but a means to get Lily's future solidified. Right?

Yeah, right, his brain snickered. *It's because of Lily, has nothing to do with the way your soul lifts when you see Mia, or the way she can make you feel that anything is possible if you try hard enough. Your chest gets tight and you can hardly breathe when that sweet scent of hers fills your nostrils because of Lily. Uh-huh.*

Caleb cleared his throat and shut off the mocking voice.

"You should come see my old place," Mia

invited, her wide grin revealing how much she approved of the changes. "It's amazing."

"What are you two whispering about in this corner?" Mayor Marsha demanded.

"We're not whispering, Mother," Caleb said.

"Yes, you were." Marsha studied him with a knowing smile. "I can always tell when you're not telling me the truth, Caleb."

"We weren't exactly whispering," Mia said. "I was about to ask Caleb if he thought your family would be available to come for Thanksgiving dinner."

"Well." Caleb choked back a laugh at Marsha's consternation. For once she seemed at a loss for words. "I, um, think we'd be delighted."

"Don't you have to check with Sis and Dad?" He kept his face as innocent looking as possible while silently cheering for Mia. He'd never known anyone to dumbfound his mother.

"I'm sure they'd love to come, but I will check with them and let you know. Will that be all right?" Marsha smiled when Mia nodded. "Good. Well, dear, I have a meeting, so I must leave. I do want to wish you all the best in your new home, though. I hope you'll be very happy."

"Thank you." Mia gracefully conceded to Marsha's effusive hug. "Your mother is a lovely woman," she said as Marsha called her goodbyes to the rest. "You're so lucky."

"Lucky?" Caleb blinked in surprise. No one had ever said that to him before.

"Yes. Lucky, or rather blessed," Mia said in a firm tone. "You could have had far less loving foster parents than the Grants. God certainly looked after you."

Mia left to speak to several others who were following Marsha's lead and leaving. Caleb mused on what she'd said.

He'd never thought of himself as lucky or blessed. Actually in his deepest heart he'd held a grudge against God for breaking up his family, for letting his mother die, for allowing his father to escape just punishment, though he'd always been glad the authorities had made sure he didn't have to live with a drunk who'd never been able to care for him. But blessed?

Years replayed in Caleb's memory of the many kids he'd met in the foster system and the horror stories of the families they'd been sent to. He'd never experienced any hardship, never needed anything. Marsha and Ben had showered him with affection from the moment he arrived. They still did. They loved him and they made sure he knew it.

What had he given them back? Duty? Obedience? He owed them much more, but that was why he couldn't keep on allowing soft thoughts for Mia to grow. Caleb couldn't love. He knew that. Lara had known that. But he didn't want Mia to know it. It would diminish him in her eyes, and Caleb so wanted to be the man she admired.

Chapter Seven

"Caleb, I need your help." Mia wished she hadn't needed to call him at his office. "Actually Meals on Wheels needs your help. It's my day to volunteer, but Abby has an emergency at work, so, well…"

She was babbling and she knew it. Caleb's generosity in organizing her housewarming still gave her a warm feeling inside. His actions had helped ease her way into making friends in Buffalo Gap. But lately she'd realized the community was pairing her with Caleb, which made her nervous and wary. She'd decided to avoid him. Until now.

"Mia? Are you there?"

"Sorry," she apologized, stuffing away her concerns. "What did you say?"

"I said I'd love to help you, but I'm due in court in ten minutes and I can't back out." He sounded rushed. "Maybe if you'd called earlier—"

"No, it's fine. Really. I'll get someone else.

Thanks anyway." She hung up before his rumbly voice could cause any more damage to her skittering nerves. Why was it that she only had to hear him speak and her insides trembled?

"Mia? Is anything wrong?" Mayor Marsha stood at her car door. "Nice," she said, admiring the vehicle Mia had finally purchased a few days earlier. "I've always loved red vehicles."

"Me, too." Mia smiled, wondering how it was that the mayor seemed to show up at just the right moment. "You wouldn't have a spare hour, would you?"

"Ah, Meals on Wheels." Marsha shook her head. "I'm sorry. I've a meeting in about five minutes. Maybe Joel could help you."

"Joel?" Mia blanked out for a minute, then followed Marsha's glance to the man sitting on a bench across the street. Caleb's dad.

"He doesn't look busy and he's been here long enough to know where most everybody lives," Marsha said. "He helped me last week with meal deliveries. Maybe you could ask him."

"But Caleb—" Mia didn't want to say it, but it seemed important to consider his aversion to his father.

"Forget Caleb. You need help, and Joel's available," Marsha said firmly. "I'll ask him if you're shy. Joel!" She waved her hand to beckon him. The older man rose, walking toward them with a quizzical look on his face.

"I'm not sure—" Mia swallowed the rest of her objections because Joel was too near.

"Mia needs help delivering meals," Marsha explained. "Are you available?"

"Yes. Nobody seems to need a handyman today." He looked directly at Mia. "Are you sure you want me to help you?"

Swallowing her reservations, she nodded. "I'd appreciate it. Otherwise I'm going to be late because I'll have to do it alone. I don't know most of the people on my list. Not yet," she said with a smile, thinking how little he seemed like the monster Caleb portrayed. "Climb in and let's go pick up the meals." While Joel got in her car Mia smiled at Marsha. "Thanks for your help."

"Have a good day," Marsha said with a nod. Was that glint in her eye satisfaction?

Mia didn't have time to dwell on it as she drove to the hospital kitchen and loaded the meals. Joel had to repeat his directions to the third house because her mind was busy noticing how easy he was to talk to. As they delivered the meals she thought how lonely Joel seemed.

"Three more and then we're finished." Mia checked the car's clock, amazed to see an hour had flown by. "I've really enjoyed this. You should add your name to the volunteer list. They could really use more people."

"I'd like to," he said quietly. "But I don't know how much longer I'll be in town."

"You have to move on?" From the downturn of his lips, Mia didn't think Joel wanted to leave Buffalo Gap.

"I haven't been able to find much work and my money's getting low." He sighed. "Turn in here." When she pulled to a stop he got out and delivered the meal.

"You were saying you didn't have work?" she prodded when he returned. If Joel left town, she felt certain he and Caleb would never reconcile and Caleb would never be rid of the anger and bitterness that had built up over the years.

"I was hoping to stay here longer." Joel glanced at her with eyes so like Caleb's. "I'd hoped to get my son to at least talk to me, but…"

"I have some jobs at Riverbend," she blurted. "I know it's autumn and probably too late to do much in the garden, but I'd like to prepare the area for some work in the spring. There's also the matter of two horses."

"You own horses?" he said with some surprise. "I didn't know you rode."

"I don't." Mia made a face. "A neighbor phoned this morning to say he'd been looking after two horses that belong to Riverbend. He's not able to do it anymore and would like them moved as soon as possible." She sighed. "I didn't know anything about horses coming with the property, but I can't just abandon them. Do you know how to look after horses?"

"I worked on a dude ranch down South for a while. I know the basics." A smile lit up Joel's face, then dissipated in his frown. "Are you sure you want to trust me to work for you? You know about my wife?"

"I know she died in tragic circumstances." Mia followed his directions to the next address. When he returned to the car, she faced him. "I know there's a wall between you and Caleb. I can't guarantee that you staying in town will help break it down but I do think it's important you keep trying."

"He'll be furious with you for hiring me." Joel's sad eyes met her. "I don't want to be the cause of a rift between you."

"Caleb is my friend. I'd like you to be my friend, too," Mia said with a smile. "But more than that, I think it's very important for both of you to find common ground. If you're at the ranch when Caleb visits, maybe he'll be forced to see the past in a different way and come to terms with it. I just want to help him, Joel."

"Thank you for caring about him," Joel said quietly.

Mia took the plunge. "You're welcome to come to Riverbend with me. I'll show you what I want you to do. There's a little bunkhouse that you could use. Once you see everything you can decide whether or not to accept my offer."

"Thank you." Were those tears in his eyes? "But if at any time you'd like me to leave, you must say so. Agreed?"

"If that's the way you want it." Satisfied, Mia drove to their final stop. With all their meals delivered, she headed for home.

Home. What a lovely word.

On the way she prayed that she was making the right decision. Caleb would be upset, but that wasn't going to stop her from doing what she could to help him reconnect.

But could You step in and ease things a bit, Lord? She shuddered at the thought of Caleb's anger turned on her. She didn't want to hurt him. He'd been good and kind to her and she liked him a lot.

Too much?

Mia reminded herself of Caleb's insistence that he couldn't love. Given his relationship with Lily, she knew he had a lot of love to give. But it wouldn't be for her. If she ever let herself trust a man enough to have a relationship, it would be to have a real marriage, with children.

And that was a dream Mia could never have. She wasn't fit to be a mother. Ever. It was too dangerous. Harlan had made sure she understood the consequences of that long-ago mistake. He'd forgiven her but Mia doubted Caleb would.

In his eyes she'd be a murderer, just like Joel.

* * *

"What, *exactly*, is going on?" Caleb glared at his father, barely able to squeeze out the words around the lump of gall lodged in his throat. "What are *you* doing here?"

"Joel's working for me," Mia said, stepping between father and son. "He's the answer to my prayers, actually."

"Some prayers," Caleb mocked. He crossed his arms across his chest as an iron band tightened inside. "Doing what?"

"Helping me with my horses, for one thing." Her joyful smile sent that familiar yet crazy warmth through his blood.

"Horses?" He listened impatiently while she explained. "Yeah, I remember old man Ness did have a couple of horses when he owned Riverbend. I didn't realize Harlan had boarded them." He faced his father. "But that doesn't explain *your* presence here."

"*I* hired him." There was a steely tone to Mia's voice that Caleb had never heard before.

So mind your own business was implicit in her words. He'd wanted Mia to stand up for herself, Caleb mused in self-mockery. He just hadn't expected she'd do it with him.

"Joel, you go over and explain that we'll take possession of the horses as soon as we can make provision for them," Mia said. "If Mr. Ness has any suggestions about which outbuildings we should use, please take note of them."

Joel nodded and left after a glance at Caleb.

"Are you sure this is a good idea?" he asked when his father was gone.

"You're the one who told me I needed to step out and live," Mia reminded him. "Or words to that effect. Now you're changing your mind?"

"No, but you also need to protect yourself," he warned. "Joel Crane will take advantage of you. That's what he does, Mia. He is not a man who deserves your pity."

"I don't feel pity. I need help. Joel can help me." Her tone changed to reproof. "Everyone deserves a second chance, Caleb."

"Haven't you learned yet to protect yourself?" Exasperated but seeing her implacability, Caleb put away his other objections for another time. He'd have to be the one to protect her from his father.

"I'm going inside for tea. Feel free to join me if you have time." Mia tossed the offer over one shoulder as she headed for the house.

"Can I have coffee? Strong coffee? I need the caffeine." Caleb followed, wondering why he'd chosen to drive out here yet knowing the answer. Mia would listen and understand. She wouldn't say something inane. She'd address his issue head-on.

Sure enough she asked, "What's wrong, Caleb?"

once the coffeemaker was dripping water through the grounds.

"You got a new coffeemaker—just for me?" He grinned, enjoying her flushed face as he sat on a stool at the breakfast bar.

"For anyone who visits and wants coffee," Mia corrected, flushing more deeply as she lowered her head to avoid looking at him. "New house, new coffeemaker. Now, what's bothering you?"

"You met Bethany, the newest girl at Family Ties?" he asked.

"Last week. She had her baby yesterday, didn't she?" Mia nodded. "I'm going to stop by tomorrow with a gift for her."

"Don't bother." When she lifted her head from arranging a plate of cookies, Caleb told her the rest. "Her parents arrived and took her and her baby boy home."

"But she was adamant about giving him for adoption when I spoke to her last." Mia studied him. "You couldn't stop it?"

"I wish I could have. She's very mature, but it turns out she's underage and they don't want their grandchild given to strangers." Caleb clamped his jaw shut, remembering Bethany's shame, pain and hurt. He should have been able to protect her.

"If they want her home, that's good, isn't it?" Mia poured his coffee and nudged the plate of cookies forward before sitting beside him.

"No. They want Bethany to keep her baby to

force her to 'face up to her sins,'" he said with disgust. "Can you imagine the life she and her child will have in such an unforgiving house, where she's reminded every moment that she's sinned and made to pay for the rest of her life?"

"It sounds horrible," Mia agreed thoughtfully.

From her look Caleb guessed she was thinking of Joel, but surely she knew his sin was far different from Bethany's. "It isn't the same as with my father," he said.

"Isn't it? Sin is sin. And God forgives." She kept a bead on him for several moments. Then suddenly a dimple appeared in one cheek. "How much underage is Bethany?"

"Three months. Why?" Mia's cunning smile shocked him. "What are you thinking?"

"I'm sure there's some follow-up legal work you have to do with Bethany," she said. When Caleb shook his head, she narrowed her gaze. "No sign-offs on a detail that necessitates a meeting where you, as her lawyer, would be duty bound to advise her that if, after three months, she still feels she can't raise her child, she could return to Family Ties? Being of legal age and all," she hinted with a wink.

"It would be hard for her to give up her baby after three months, but if that's what she truly wanted—" He mulled it over, then grinned. For the first time that day, Caleb felt as if the sun had come out. But then that was always the effect Mia had on him.

"Well?" she asked, tongue in cheek.

"I do believe there is one detail I overlooked," he murmured. "As an officer of the court, I'd be remiss to let that pass. I must speak to Bethany privately."

"Good." Mia sipped her tea, but from the way she peered into the amber liquid, it was clear she something else bothered her.

"What's wrong?"

"I was at our quilting group this morning, which, by the way, I love. They asked me to design a Christmas quilt to be raffled off. We're all working on it communally and it is going to be gorgeous."

"Uh-huh." Caleb was utterly out of his depth.

"Anyway, we talk as we stitch and this morning the talk was about Lily and some new tests she had." Mia looked at him reproachfully. "You didn't tell me."

"I didn't want to say anything until I got some more answers." Caleb kept his eyes on his coffee mug. He didn't want to tell her the rest.

"What is it, Caleb? Is there anything to be done for her?"

He loved the concern in Mia's voice for the little girl he adored.

"Caleb?" Maybe it was the weight of her hand on his arm, or the gentleness of her question, or perhaps it was the glow of her emerald eyes. Whatever the reason, it suddenly became easy for Caleb to reveal his heart.

"There is something that can be done for Lily," he said carefully. "There is a specialist who comes to Calgary who could see her, but he's not scheduled for a visit there for another three months, and the cost of his work is not covered by our government health care plan."

"Money is not the issue here, Caleb. Lily must have the best we can get, no matter what the cost." Mia pulled forward a pad of paper and a pen. "What is this surgeon's name?"

"Dr. Peter Frank. But, Mia, he won't make a special trip just for—"

"Have some faith, Caleb." She grinned at him and then, to his amazement, winked. "One of the members in my Calgary church was a doctor whose son was in my Sunday-school class. I'm going to talk to him and see if he can help us."

Caleb watched Mia make her phone call, hardly daring to hope. Yesterday he'd been defeated by the information he received about Lily, certain there was little more he could do. But as Mia spoke to her friend, a flicker of hope flamed to life. Despite his intention to remain unmoved by the lovely textile artist, his appreciation of Mia and her refusal to take no when it came to Lily's welfare soared. How could he ever have thought Mia fragile?

As she crossed each barrier in reaching her goal to speak to Dr. Frank, Caleb realized how much had changed in the shy, reticent woman he'd met a few months ago. Or maybe her determination had always been there. Whatever it was, Caleb was inordinately glad that he hadn't walked away that first day he'd met Mia.

Several times Caleb noticed Mia's eyes close when she was put on hold. He realized she was praying. Mia's faith in God's love for His children continually intrigued Caleb. Unlike him, she seemed to have no questions about God. Caleb envied her that. He'd seen her gentle, loving manner win over crotchety folks at church and bitter young women at Family Ties. Nobody was immune to Mia's warmth.

Including him? Most of all him, Caleb's heart insisted.

Within half an hour Mia was speaking personally to Dr. Frank, laying out Lily's case before asking him to make a special concession to see her. Caleb couldn't tell from her face after she hung up the phone what the decision was.

"Well?" he asked impatiently when she doodled on her notepad.

"He'll see her, but only if we can get her to Sick Kids Hospital in Toronto by Friday." Mia's calm pronouncement stunned Caleb.

"Friday?" He blinked. "But—that's only three days from now."

"So we'd better get to work." Mia shot him a grin, then pulled forward her laptop and punched in an airline's website. Fingers hovering above the keyboard, she turned to him and asked, "You are coming, aren't you?"

"Oh, I'm coming," he assured her, reaching for his wallet. "You can charge our two tickets on my card."

"Two? You don't think I'd let that little girl go without me, do you?" Mia glared at him. "I will be with Lily through whatever comes, Caleb. Don't even try to stop me."

"I wasn't going to," he said, delighted by her response. Mia ignored his outstretched card.

"Thank you, but not necessary." She kept her eyes on her keyboard. "I guess this is a good time to tell you. I have set up a trust fund for Lily."

Caleb felt bemused, befuddled, as if he'd missed something. "You did?"

"Well, actually Bella did, at my request. It will cover any expenses we incur." She did look at him then. "Of course, you'll have to sign off on the expenses because you'll be the administrator."

"But—" He struggled to find words. This woman. This marvelous, wonderful woman. Caleb's heart expanded until he could hardly breathe. "Mia, that's so kind of you. It's amazing." Her generosity toward Lily humbled him. "Are you sure you want to use your personal funds—"

"They're not *my* funds. That glass you found

in my basement turned out to be genuine Lalique and worth quite a bit." She chuckled when his eyes opened wide. "I loved four of those pieces, so I kept them. They're displayed in my bedroom."

"And the rest?" he asked, hardly daring to believe he'd finally achieved his goal for Lily.

"Bella contacted an art dealer friend who was delighted to find homes in museums for the most special pieces. The rest were sold. That's Lily's fund. Bella will get the information to you as soon as everything is settled." Mia told him the amount.

Caleb's jaw dropped in shock. Mia returned to booking the airline tickets, then paused. "Do you think Hilda should come along?"

"No. She hates flying. The man she was once engaged to died piloting an airplane. She hasn't flown since." Caleb still couldn't believe it. "Mia, are you sure?"

"Yes." She looked across the breakfast bar at something he couldn't see. "I've prayed for weeks about that glass. Harlan meant its use for something else, but God had other plans. Harlan's rare old books were sold to set up a fund for needy women who come to Family Ties." She shrugged. "You'll have to administer that, too, I'm afraid. Along with Abby, of course."

Caleb couldn't find the words. Mia had taken a negative in her life, her husband's miserly trick against her, and turned it into something wonderful.

"You know that verse 'All things work together

for good'?" she asked, face upturned. "Well, I believe that's what God is doing in my life. He's working things out. Like this ranch, like your dad helping me, like providing funds for Lily and helping Abby's outreach at Family Ties. It's all part of His plan."

Caleb blinked. What could he say to that? Nothing but a heartfelt thank-you.

They spent the next hour planning details like which hotel would be easiest to reach from the hospital and whether they should stay an extra day to let Lily relax. No detail seemed too small to escape Mia's attention. By the time darkness had fallen and the aroma of roasting chicken filled the kitchen, Caleb knew that if ever he could love someone, he'd want that person to be Mia.

But then his father returned and Caleb put away those wayward thoughts. Love wasn't for him— he knew that. But when had he begun to long for the right to hug Mia close, to grasp her hand and share her joy in planning wonderful things for the future?

Even if he could let go of the past, Caleb was pretty sure Mia couldn't be part of his future.

Chapter Eight

Determined not to let Lily fret over the visit with Dr. Frank, Mia kept the little girl busy with games and puzzles during the flight to Toronto.

"You thought of everything," Caleb said when Lily's head nodded onto his shoulder and she fell asleep. "She hasn't had time to worry."

"That was the goal." Mia tucked the computer Lily had used in her bag.

"It hasn't stopped me worrying," Caleb admitted. "What happens if he can't do anything for her? What if—"

"Caleb." Mia reached across Lily and threaded her hand in his. The touch made her stomach wobble, but she held on anyway. This was not the time to let her personal feelings get in the way. This was the time to join together and support this little girl. "This morning I read a scripture. 'The Lord will provide.' Let's hang on to that."

He squeezed her hand. "I am continually shamed by the strength of your faith."

"Shamed?" she asked, pleased by the compliment but too aware of her own personal struggles to trust God, of her ache to hold her own child when she knew that wasn't His will. "Part of being in God's family means supporting each other."

Mia drew her hand away. Contact with Caleb always made her wish for more, but she simply couldn't imagine ever again depending on another man. It felt utterly humiliating to remember how she'd been hoodwinked by Harlan and hadn't even suspected it, to recall her blind obedience to his edicts as if she had no mind of her own when all the time he'd been using her to get the inheritance her mother had left. Bella had summarized the totality of his nefarious schemes on the phone last night, leaving Mia feeling stupidly naive.

But at least she'd learned from her miserable marriage. She'd learned to listen to the still, small voice inside her. She'd learned to ask questions, a lot of questions, and to look for answers from more than one person. Most of all she'd learned that the freedom of choice was worthy of staying independent. So far anyway.

"Wake up, sweetheart. We're landing now." Caleb brushed Lily's cheek with his knuckles and smiled when her long dark lashes lifted. "Is your seat belt fastened?"

"Uh-huh." Lily peered at him, trust glowing in her dark blue eyes. "Will it hurt, Uncle Caleb?"

"I don't think it will hurt today. The doctor just wants to look at your leg to see if he can help you," Caleb explained.

"What if he can't, Uncle Caleb?"

Mia's heart broke as shadows moved into Caleb's silver eyes. He opened his mouth but clearly had no words, so when he looked to her, she smiled at him and then Lily.

"You mean what if he can't fix your leg?" Mia said softly.

Lily nodded. "I'll be the same then, won't I?" she asked.

"I don't know. None of knows what God has planned for us, honey." Mia cupped the child's chin in her palm. "Six months ago I didn't even imagine I'd be living at Riverbend. But God had other plans. We have to trust that He'll do what's best for us because He loves us so much. Can you do that?" she asked as the plane taxied to the terminal.

"I'll try." Lily's shoulders straightened.

Mia's heart bumped with pride as the little girl moved regally down the aisle and out of the plane. Though people turned to watch her, it wasn't her limp they were looking at. It was Lily's beautiful smile. Most of them smiled back.

So did Dr. Frank. It took less than half an hour to reach the hospital thanks to a very capable cab driver. They were immediately shown into a room where Dr. Frank probed and pressed, assessing everything with shrewd eyes as he teased Lily with a bunch of goofy jokes. When he was finished he didn't send Lily from the room as Mia had anticipated. She moved closer to Caleb, seeking his support as they waited.

"Well, Miss Lily." Dr. Frank sat in a chair, putting his eye level even with hers. "You've had some problems with your leg since you broke it, haven't you?"

"That's why we came to see you," Lily said. "Can you fix my leg, Dr. Frank?"

"I'm not sure." Mia listened intently as Dr. Frank explained how the bones had grown together wrong. "It would take a lot of operating to take the bones apart and put them back together the right way," he warned.

"That would hurt." Lily paled.

"It will hurt for a while, until your bones get used to being in the new way," Dr. Frank said honestly.

"And then I wouldn't limp?" Lily asked. "I hate limping."

"I think if we did the operation, you wouldn't limp as much, but I can't say for sure that you wouldn't limp at all, Lily." Dr. Frank leaned back in his chair. "We won't know that till after the operation."

"How much would it hurt?" Fear filled Lily's

voice. Mia moved to comfort her, but Dr. Frank made a motion that asked her to stay where she was.

"It would hurt a lot at first," he said quietly. "We would give you some medicine to make it hurt less, but it will hurt. And it will hurt while you learn to walk."

"I already know how to walk," Lily said indignantly.

"Yes, now you do, but after the operation your leg has to learn all over again. It won't want to." Dr. Frank explained every detail, answered every question to prepare Lily for what lay ahead.

Mia's head whirled. She couldn't imagine how Lily was able to understand it all, but to her surprise, the child sat straight and tall, paying close attention. Caleb looked just as focused.

"So what do you think, Lily?" Dr. Frank finally asked. "Do you think you want to have the operation on your leg or are you afraid it will hurt too much?"

Lily's forehead furrowed as she considered what he'd said. Mia wanted to go to her and lend support, but she knew it was important that the little girl make this decision herself. If Lily asked for help, she and Caleb would gladly offer it. But the choice was Lily's.

"My mom died. That hurt a lot." A tear trickled down her velvet cheek. "It still hurts."

"It probably always will," Dr. Frank said in a soft voice. "But after a while it will get easier."

And so it went. Lily asked every question she could think of and Dr. Frank patiently answered each, repeating if he needed to, easing her fears but making no attempt to mask the truth. Mia felt as though she were on pins and needles, waiting for the little girl to make her decision. At last Lily stretched out a hand toward her. Mia stepped forward and clasped it tightly. On Lily's other side Caleb did the same.

"What should I do, Mia?" Lily asked.

"I can't tell you that, honey." Mia brushed her hair off her forehead. "I can only tell you that I think Dr. Frank is very good at operating and I believe he would do his very best for you. Do you want some time to think it over and pray about it?"

"No." Lily shook her head. "I already prayed. A lot."

"Then, what does your heart say?" Mia asked softly.

"It says yes," she said firmly. "Is that okay, Uncle Caleb?"

"It's very okay." Caleb drew them both into the security of his arms. Mia could have stayed there forever, but there were details to see to. Besides, if she stayed tucked in his embrace for much longer, it would only be more painful to leave and harder to resist the craving to return to that weakling she'd been and allow someone else to be strong for her.

That could not happen. She focused on Lily.

"When?" Mia asked the doctor.

"I'd like to do the surgery as soon as possible, and I'd rather do it in Calgary," Dr. Frank said to them. "That way Lily won't have to go through a long return flight. And she'll be closer to her friends during her recovery. I know she has a lot of those." He and Lily shared a smile, but then his face grew serious. "It will be quite costly," he warned in a low voice. "I'll gladly donate my fees to help her, but the hospital will require payment for the specialized care Lily will require, and they'll want a large part of the payment up front."

"Cost is not a barrier," Mia said firmly. "Lily must have whatever she needs."

"Are you sure?" He named a figure that made Caleb's eyes widen. Mia only nodded.

"Whatever," she insisted, certain that the money she'd set aside for Lily's future could not find a better use. "Do you have a date in mind?"

"Wednesday next week." Dr. Frank smiled at her surprise. "That is, provided Calgary can set it up. It has to be then because I'll be leaving for a mission trip to Africa after Christmas and I want Lily well on the way to recovery before I go."

"Is next Wednesday okay for the operation, Lily?" Mia watched as fear fought faith in Lily's dark blue eyes. "That gives us lots of time to pray," she whispered in the child's ear. When Lily nodded, Mia hugged her.

"Will you be with me, Mia? You and Uncle Caleb?" she asked in a wobbly voice.

"Of course we'll be there. The nurses will probably have to throw us out of the hospital we'll be there so much." Mia let out a pent-up breath as Lily giggled. A glance at Caleb revealed tears glossing his eyes. When he turned his head to brush them away, Mia felt that pinch on her heart again. He was such a good man.

"Okay, I'll set it up and send you the details." Dr. Frank tweaked Lily's nose. "I'll be checking on you. You have email?" He pretended amazement when she said no. "Well, you'll have to get it. I can't go without talking to my favorite patient for a whole week!"

"I can borrow Mia's computer," Lily assured him. "Or Uncle Caleb's. They both look after me."

"You're a pretty lucky little girl to have such good people caring for you, Lily." Dr. Frank rose. "I have to go. You keep praying." His glance included all of them. "I like knowing God's been asked to attend my operations."

"I'll pray really hard," Lily promised.

"Me, too." Dr. Frank beckoned Caleb into the hallway, leaving Mia with Lily.

Although she yearned to hear what was being said, Mia accepted that as Lily's guardian, Caleb was in charge. She waited until after lunch. They walked to a nearby park where Lily could play. Then Mia asked what had been said in the hallway at the hospital.

"Dr. Frank shared some details about her aftercare," he told her. "I'm concerned about that. I don't think Ms. Hilda can manage everything."

"I've noticed she's getting less mobile. Why is that?" Mia asked.

"Hilda fell last year and reinjured her knee when she was looking after the son of a friend of mine, a little boy named Henry. The doctors recommended Hilda have a knee replacement this fall, but then Lily needed a place to stay and…" He let the rest of it trail away.

Mia knew what was coming, but she also knew it couldn't happen. She steeled herself against his anxious voice.

"You've already done so much, Mia. I hate to ask this. But would it be possible for you to have Lily stay at your place to recuperate—"

She had to stop him.

"I'd like nothing more than for Lily to come to Riverbend, Caleb. Goodness knows I certainly have the room. But I can't do it." She turned her head away from his probing gaze and studied the little girl working so hard to climb up the stairs to the slide. "It just isn't possible. I'm sorry."

"Can you tell me why?" His voice, soft, patient, soothed that part inside her that yearned for tenderness. "Please? I won't judge."

Perhaps that promise was why Mia gave in to the urge to tell the story she'd kept secreted inside for five long years.

"You call your father a murderer," she began. "Well, I am, too. I'm responsible for a child's death. He's dead because of me." There—she'd said it. Mia looked at Caleb, steeling herself for the disgust and loathing she knew she'd see there.

But Caleb's silver-gray eyes held neither disgust nor abhorrence, only surprise and compassion mixed with sadness. He glanced over to make sure Lily was all right, then lifted Mia's hand and folded it into his.

"Tell me what happened, Mia." His kindness was her undoing.

"His name was Bobby Janzen," she said, unable to stop the gush of words or tears. "He was three years old and I loved him."

Harlan had never let her explain, never wanted to hear the details of that horrible time. He'd "cleaned up her mess," as he'd put it, then forbade her to ever babysit another child again. He couldn't afford the scandal of her ineptitude, he'd said.

"Go on." Caleb tightened his grip on her hand when she would have pulled away. "Lily's chatting with that little boy," he said when she glanced away. "She's fine. Tell me the rest of the story."

"Bobby's parents were our neighbors," Mia explained after a deep breath. "I was bored that first year I was married to Harlan. I was used to school and people and things filling my day. Then my mother was gone and there was nothing but grief. I had to do something, and since Harlan didn't want me to work, I started going to the park. I met Bobby." She closed her eyes and let the memories fill her mind.

"You befriended him?"

"Yes. He was a darling child. I never got tired of sketching him. I gave him one. His parents thanked me for it." Her voice wobbled. Mia paused to regain control. "After a while his nanny and I would meet in the park. When she'd chat about him I'd soak in every detail. That little boy held my heart in his hands. I'd have done anything for him."

"Something happened." There was no question in Caleb's voice.

"One day his nanny told me it was her last day caring for Bobby," Mia said softly. "She was getting married, moving away."

"So you took over for her." Caleb nodded. "Understandable."

"Not exactly." Mia shook her head. "Harlan would never have agreed to that. But I did begin babysitting Bobby at night, when his parents wanted to go out. They'd always have him ready for bed. All I had to do was give him his bottle and tuck him in." She stopped, suddenly grief filled at the memory of holding that sweet, warm child and singing to him, of knowing he'd never smile or chortle that funny laugh of his again. The pain never went away.

"Say it, Mia." Caleb put an arm around her shoulder and drew her against his side. "What happened?"

"I didn't put him to bed right." She choked out the words. "I thought I had. But when I went to check on him an hour after I put him down he wasn't breathing. Harlan told me later that Bobby had choked and died because I wasn't careful enough," she whispered, heart wrenching at the memory.

"Careful enough? But he wasn't an infant," Caleb said with a frown. "So…?"

"I'd given Bobby a little bear for Christmas. He was always rubbing it against his face. It was soft and it made a little noise." She gulped at the memory of Bobby's joy in the silly little gift. "Usually the bear sat on his nightstand, but that night he was fussing and I let him take it to bed with him. Harlan said the bear came apart and he choked on a part. Bobby died because of me, Caleb. I gave him the toy and then let him have it in bed. It was only because Harlan pleaded with Bobby's parents that I wasn't charged with his death."

"So now you won't be alone with any child," Caleb's lips murmured against her hair.

"I can't allow it." Mia turned to look at him, surprised to find his face so near hers. "That's the promise I made Bobby's parents. Harlan said it was the reason they didn't have me charged with his death. I had to promise I'd never be in a position to endanger another young child."

"Oh, Mia, what a lot of grief you've carried." Both Caleb's arms went around her then. His lips pressed against her forehead. "I know you'd never hurt a child. I'm so sorry this happened to you."

"So am I." How wonderful to be held so tenderly, to feel his touch against her skin. Caleb hadn't reacted at all as she'd expected. Maybe he didn't understand. Hating to break contact, she drew back so she could gaze into his eyes. "I would love to have Lily stay with me, but I can't, Caleb. I will never put another child in danger."

Caleb could hardly stand the grief in her voice. "Mia, Lily's older. She won't choke. She—" But Mia interrupted him.

"What if she fell and I wasn't there to catch her?" She turned her head to study the little girl. "What if she climbed to the top of that slide at Riverbend and somehow fell off?"

"That wouldn't be your fault!"

"Yes, Caleb, it would, because I'd have broken my promise." She bit her lip as one lonely tear dribbled down her cheek. "I know God has forgiven me, but I can't forgive myself."

Caleb tried to argue, but he could see his protests did no good. Mia had lived with her guilt for far too long. She explained that she loved children, hence her Sunday-school class at the Calgary church, but that there had always been others there to make sure nothing happened.

Somehow the more Mia explained, the more a feeling grew inside him, a kind of hunch that Harlan had somehow used Bobby's death to keep Mia bound to him and that ugly house she'd lived in. Guilt and fear were the perfect tools to stop activities he didn't control.

"I'll do anything I can for Lily. I love her very much." Mia rose. Her gaze slid from the child to him, determination lifting her chin. "But I can't keep her at Riverbend."

There was no more time for discussion because Lily came over limping wearily. Caleb treated both his ladies to a special dinner, but after they returned to their suite at the hotel, both Mia and Lily seemed subdued and soon retired to their rooms. Left alone in the living room, Caleb phoned Marsha. Ever since that day so long ago when he'd first met her as a foster child, she'd been there for him. Now he needed her advice.

True to form, Marsha listened carefully to everything he had to say.

"The operation is wonderful news, dear. How amazing that Mia would do that for Lily. Such a sweet woman. But why do you think she won't take Lily to Riverbend?"

"It was a personal confidence, Mother. I can't

say." Caleb would not betray Mia's trust in him. "Let's just say she's afraid to be alone with Lily in case something happens."

"Then, it seems to me your path is clear." Caleb could almost see Marsha's eyes glow as her firm voice transmitted into his ear. "You need to find someone who will stay at Riverbend with Mia. Perhaps then she'll reconsider."

"Maybe." The more he thought about it, the more Caleb believed that was his answer. "But who?"

"Ordinarily I'd have a dozen names for you," Marsha said in a troubled tone. "But half the church has signed up for that gospel cruise with Pastor Don. It starts next week. I don't think most of those left would be much help with an invalid child. I'd offer, but your father is so looking forward to our yearly trip to Montana that I'd hate to see him disappointed. Still," she said, "if it's a matter of a child's health—"

"No, Marsha. You have a hectic schedule. You and Dad need that time away together. I'll think of someone. Oh, I know. Ms. Hilda." Caleb barely had a moment to savor his solution before his mother ended that.

"I heard via the grapevine today that the doctors are pressing her to get that knee operation as soon as possible," Marsha said quietly. "She's put it off because of Lily, but it's getting to the state where she needs to have it done or..."

"So we've got two folks who need care." Caleb sighed, frustrated by the news.

"Seems to me you need to seek the Lord's help on this one, son. That's my best advice." Marsha caught him up on some other local news, but Caleb knew the odd silences interspersing her words were because Marsha was yawning.

"Thanks, Mom. Get some sleep. I'll see you tomorrow."

"Caleb, have you spoken with your father?" By her tone he knew she was referring to Joel.

"I have nothing to say to him." He couldn't help the anger in those words.

"As long as you keep that attitude, you'll never be able to move on," Marsha said in a gently reproving voice. "And I think you need to move on, don't you?"

"What do you mean?" he asked, confused by her words.

"There's a certain widow newly moved into Riverbend for whom you seem to have great affection. Don't make the same mistake you made with Lara, Caleb. Don't let anger over your past ruin what could be something special with Mia. Good night, dear. I'll be praying." Marsha hung up before he could respond.

Caleb sat in the dark room overlooking Toronto's night sky, musing on her words. Did he have a special fondness for Mia? Of course. The remembered pleasure of holding her in his arms kept intruding, though he tried to suppress it.

In the silence of the night he began to examine what lay behind his need to make sure Mia didn't feel alone, why Caleb wanted to be there for her, to make sure each moment in her life was filled with the joy she'd been denied too long.

It wasn't because he loved her, though some strong emotion inside flared whenever she was near. But that wasn't love.

Was it?

Chapter Nine

"We'll be right here waiting for you." Caleb bent and pressed a kiss against Lily's cheek, ignoring the others gathered around the little girl in her hospital room. Mia's heart squeezed as emotion overwhelmed him. He couldn't say the words, but there was no doubt he loved this child.

"We'll be praying, sweetheart," she whispered in Lily's ear, then relinquished her grip of the small hand as the nurses wheeled Lily's gurney from the room. "We love you."

"Love you, too" came the drowsy response.

And then she was gone and Mia was alone with Caleb.

"I hate this," he said, his jaw clenched tight. His hand sought hers and held on as if it were a lifeline.

"Of course you do. So do I. Because we're not in control." She smiled at the teddy bears and balloons that so many from Buffalo Gap had sent to encourage Lily.

"Dr. Frank better be as good as his reputation," Caleb growled.

"We're not depending on Dr. Frank. Our trust is in God." Mia couldn't sit in this empty room and wait. She needed to move. "Let's go for a walk."

"But—"

"He said at least four hours, Caleb." She tugged on his hand. "There's nothing we can do here. Come on."

After a bit more persuasion Caleb agreed to leave Lily's room. In the crisp autumn sunshine, Mia drew in deep breaths, trying to quell the sense of worry plaguing her. A passage from Isaiah's thirtieth chapter filled her thoughts. "The Lord will be very gracious to you at the sound of your cry." *I'm crying to You, Lord*, she prayed silently. *Please help Lily.*

"It's going to snow soon." Caleb lifted his face into the light breeze.

"How can you tell?" Mia matched her step to his until he realized she was almost running and modulated his pace.

"Believe it or not, it's the one good thing my old man taught me before he screwed up my life." Caleb's fingers tightened on hers. She squeezed back. He turned his head and grinned at her. "Too tight? Sorry."

"Tell me about this thing Joel taught you." She wanted him to dwell on this first positive thing she'd ever heard him say about Joel. "Can Ben do it, too?"

"No. Ben is a born rancher, but he could never sense a weather change the way I can." Caleb shook his head. "My dad's better at it than me, though. He doesn't even have to stick his head outside. Somehow the barometric pressure changes and Joel just knows what's coming. I can't explain it."

"That's amazing." Mia pointed out a cloud formation over the tips of the distant Rockies. "Looks as if you're right. Joel isn't just good at weather, though. He's also amazing with Lily. She says he's building a rocking horse for her. She's ecstatic that I own horses. You do know she wants to ride again?"

"I know, and it scares me to death." Caleb let go of her hand and wrapped his arm around her waist, drawing her closer as a strong wind began to buffet them. "Sure you want to keep walking in this?"

"Yes. I like facing off against the elements." And she liked being so close to him, protected, cherished. Where was her hard-won independence now, Mia asked herself. "Did Joel ever make toys for you?" she asked, hoping to draw on his pleasant memories.

"He once carved a train set for me for Christmas. I guess he and Mom couldn't afford the real thing, so he made it out of wood. Really intricate work," he remembered, his voice far away. Silence fell between them because the wind gusts made it difficult to speak. Caleb pointed to a fast food place across the street. "Let's go have coffee. Or tea," he added with a grimace.

"Joel's also a great Bible teacher," Mia said, continuing the conversation when they were both seated with a hot drink. "The other day I mentioned Martha—you know the story about Mary and Martha, the two sisters who Jesus visited?"

"You mean the Martha who felt she was doing all the work while Mary enjoyed Jesus's visit? Yeah, I know it." Caleb frowned. "What does Joel have to do with it?"

"I never understood why Jesus rebuked Martha. I've always thought she got the short end of the stick, that she slaved away and her lazy sister let her." Mia chuckled. "Joel helped me see that when Jesus rebuked Martha it wasn't because she was working too hard or that He didn't appreciate it. It was because her focus was wrong. He offered her a golden opportunity to hear what He had to say and instead she focused on trivial things to show she was a good hostess. Joel gave me a new perspective on relationships with God."

"He should practice what he preaches." The hardness in Caleb's voice made her wince.

"He's trying, Caleb. He's really trying to put

the past behind him and make his life count," Mia said gently.

"That's too easy. It lets him forget my mom," Caleb snapped.

"He hasn't forgotten, Caleb. She's constantly in his thoughts. 'My wife was a great baker,' he told me the other day when I made an apple pie. And he mentioned that she would have enjoyed our quilting group." Mia nodded. "In fact, he speaks of her often."

"That doesn't change what he did," Caleb said coldly.

"Are you sure he's guilty of murder?" Mia couldn't let it rest. Somehow she had to help Caleb let this go. Maybe if he could get past the barriers...

"Are you sure he isn't?" Caleb's glare pinned her in place. "I was there. I saw it happen. He pushed her."

"Or he reached out and she backed away." He didn't like that, evidenced by the flare of anger in his eyes. Mia tried again. "Or perhaps he did reach out to push her away as she advanced on him. And perhaps that's why she fell. Or perhaps— What does it matter now, Caleb? It won't bring your mother back."

"Exactly." He crossed his arms over his chest and leaned back, jaw rock hard.

"Joel told me your mother was a godly woman."

Mia decided to try one last time. "Wouldn't she have forgiven him if he'd asked?"

The nerve in Caleb's left cheek twitched as he worked to control his resentment. Strangely Mia didn't feel afraid. She only felt sympathy. Well, she also felt a deep desperate need to wrap her arms around him and hold him close, taking his pain.

If only she could. Because she loved him.

The self-realization stunned Mia so much she barely heard him say they needed to return to the hospital. It took Caleb pointing out the tiny snowflakes for her to notice that the sun had disappeared and winter was on its way.

You can't love Caleb. It's a mistake to let any man get close. He'll want to tell you what to do, try to bend you to his will, just as Harlan did. He might even try to trick you to adopt Lily. You can't love him.

"Why is it so important to you that I forgive my father, Mia?" As they walked into the hospital, Caleb's quiet question drew her from her introspection.

She stared at him, mentally noting all the things she most admired about him. He was tall and strong and principled. He had integrity that he wasn't willing to breach. He loved Lily, did everything he could to make sure her life would get better. Almost everything.

"If you could forgive your father…" she began,

feeling her way as she spoke. "If the two of you could come together, reunite your family—" She stopped. Dared she say it?

"Not going to happen," he insisted firmly. Then he lifted one eyebrow. "But say it did. So what? Why does this matter to you?"

"Because it would make you happy," she whispered, staring at him. "It would end your self-imposed suffering. And Joel's. The two of you could find some common ground."

"And?" he pressed when she hesitated.

"Then you could make a home for Lily," Mia said in a rush.

Caleb's eyes stretched wide in astonishment. He stared at her, blinked, clearly stunned. Finally he shook his head.

"Also not going to happen, Mia. But let me ask the same of you. When are you going to get past your fear? When will you stop letting what Harlan said and did affect the rest of your life?"

"I'm trying to do that," she whispered.

"Are you?" His eyes seemed to drill into her, exposing her secrets. "So when are you going to let go of your guilt over Bobby and adopt Lily as your own child? You are meant to be a mother."

The thought of it was so attractive that Mia got caught up in imagining all the things she and Lily could do together. Funny how Caleb always figured into those plans. It took a moment to remember it couldn't happen.

"I'm rebuilding my life the best I can." A sense of vulnerability swept over her. "I'm trying to break through all the barriers Harlan caused."

"Are you enjoying your new life?" he asked.

"Of course I love having my own home where I can indulge my style. I love having my own car and driving where I want to go." She exhaled and glared at him. "I know you think there's nothing to stop me from doing all the things I've only dreamed of except my fear, but that fear is as real to me as your hatred toward your father."

"I don't hate him," Caleb said, but she ignored him.

"I wish that one day I could have a child of my own." Mia saw his eyes flare and knew what he was hoping, but she had to dash those hopes. "I wish that so much. But that's not going to happen. It can't."

"Why?" Caleb followed her into Lily's empty room. When she stood by the window and didn't respond, he took her arm, forcing her to face him. "Why can't you be a mother?"

"Because I couldn't survive if something happened," she murmured, heart aching. She loved the way his silver eyes softened when they looked at her, thrilled to the touch of his fingers as they sought out her hand and held it.

With Caleb near she felt strong, capable. But Caleb wouldn't always be there. She had to depend on herself.

"You're stronger than you think, Mia," he murmured. "And I don't believe you'd ever let anything happen to a child." His arms slid around her waist and he drew her close. "You're too full of love."

Even through her coat Mia could feel the strength in him, solid and dependable. She needed that strength right now, needed desperately to make him understand. For a moment she gave in to her heart's yearning and laid her head against his chest, relishing the tenderness she had not known in six years of marriage.

"I love Lily with all my heart, Caleb. If I had a daughter, I'd want her to be exactly like that little girl." She lifted her head just enough to gaze into his eyes. "What will we do if—"

"She's going to be fine," he said, his lips millimeters from hers. "God wouldn't let anything happen to a sweet kid like Lily. Have faith, Mia." Then his face moved those few millimeters and his mouth touched hers.

Mia had only ever been kissed twice in high school. She didn't know exactly how to return his embrace. All she did know was that when his lips pressed against hers, joy suffused her. She wanted to show him how much she enjoyed his touch, how deeply moved she was. So she kissed him back as best she knew how, thrilled that he didn't pull away but instead drew her even closer.

She savored every moment, every tiny detail,

tucking them into her memory to take out and think about later. Mia wanted that kiss to go on and on, but too soon Caleb drew his lips away. A sense of loss filled her until his big hand snuggled her face against his chest once more.

She could stay here forever, Mia thought, safe in his strong yet tender embrace.

He shouldn't have kissed her, Caleb told himself over and over as he and Mia waited in Lily's room. Mia was inexperienced. She wouldn't understand he'd only been trying to comfort her.

Comfort her or yourself? He shoved the thought away, but his mind immediately drifted to the pleasure he'd found in holding Mia, in letting her lean on him. When he'd finally found enough sense to draw away, her eyes were sparkling, her face shining, and he knew he had to be very careful not to let Mia expect more from him. He couldn't love her. He didn't know how to love.

For the tenth time he checked his watch. Lily had been in surgery for three hours. His whole body clenched when there was a movement by the door. Something had gone wrong. He didn't know whether to groan or grit his teeth when his father walked in.

"I wanted to stay away," Joel said quietly. "But I couldn't. Is there any news?"

Caleb was about to tell Joel to leave but Mia rose and walked toward him. She hugged him.

"Not yet. Come and wait with us," she invited. "We can pray together."

Caleb couldn't watch his father fawn over Mia, fooling her as he seemed to have done to everyone else. He jumped to his feet.

"I'm going to get some coffee," he said, and stalked from the room. But the hospital cafeteria was noisy and he couldn't sort out his thoughts there so he left, searching for some place to be alone, to sort out his miasma of feelings.

There was no one inside the chapel. Soft ambient lighting gave no hint to the time of day. Hymns hummed in the background, enfolding Caleb in their comforting sound. A stained glass window sat center front, its words backlit.

"As I have loved you…you also love one another."

It wasn't a plea or a request. It was an order. Love one another. The question was, how could Caleb love a man he was convinced had killed his mother?

Wouldn't your mother have forgiven him? Mia had asked. And that was the thing. His mom would have, instantly and completely. She'd loved Joel with every fiber of her being. She'd told Caleb that, shown it in every word, every action toward Joel.

"I can't do it," he whispered. And yet he had to. The anger that continually festered inside was eating him up, ruining his life. Caleb knew it could not go on. "Show me how to forgive," he prayed.

His eyes strayed to the right. Another verse, smaller and less conspicuous hung from a tapestry. *Forgetting those things which are behind, I press on toward the goal.*

The apostle Paul had done awful things. And yet God had forgiven him. How could He have done that?

His mother's favorite verse, which she'd framed and hung on her bedroom wall, suddenly filled his mind. *My grace is sufficient for you.*

Meaning what? That if God could forgive, Caleb had to accept that and move on. Meaning he needed to forgive and move on? Could he do that?

Every fiber of his being yearned to be free of the load of anger he'd carried for so long. And yet—

Caleb checked his watch, then rose to leave. He found himself looking directly into the painted gaze of Jesus holding a child on His knee. The artist had depicted such love in His intense eyes that for a moment Caleb couldn't look away.

"I'll try to forgive him," he promised finally, then left the quiet room. But what to do about Mia?

When Caleb arrived at Lily's room, the door was open. Quiet voices spilled out to him. He stood in the hallway, hesitant to interrupt.

"Mia, being content does not mean being complacent as you were before." His father's voice floated toward Caleb. "It doesn't mean being wary about everyone, either. You trusted your husband. That's what wives are supposed to do. The fault was in him. You can't make up for his faults by protecting yourself, by never caring for anyone again."

Mia murmured something Caleb couldn't hear.

"If only I could change the past, go back to that day and have my wife alive again." Could the sorrow in Joel's words be faked? Caleb wondered. "I'd give my life for hers if I could. But that's not the way it is. I made a terrible mistake. God has forgiven me. I only wish Caleb could."

"I'm not sure I've forgiven Harlan, Joel." As Caleb listened, Mia's voice broke. She cleared her throat and continued, "I wanted my mother's love so badly, but I felt like a nuisance to her. So I tried to stay out of her way even though I was so lonely. Then I married Harlan and I felt just as abandoned. It was so hard to keep trusting God."

"But you did and now here you are." Joel's voice softened. "You've come through the clouds into the light and now you can look to your future with hope. You can pass on what you've learned to Lily."

"I love Lily." The wistfulness in Mia's squeezed Caleb's heart. "Caleb thinks I should adopt her, but I can't."

"Because of Bobby Janzen," his father said. So Mia had told Joel about the little boy who died? She must really trust him.

"His death has never left me. I was responsible for that. If I hadn't been so careless…" A sound puzzled him until he realized it was Mia weeping.

The heartbreak of her sorrow hit Caleb hard. There had to be something he could do to help her. Maybe she hadn't understood everything. Maybe Harlan had lied about the circumstances. He pulled out his phone and texted his paralegal, asking her to find out everything she could about a three-year-old child named Bobby Janzen who'd died less than six years ago. He couldn't love Mia, but maybe he could help her.

Caleb had just completed his call when someone touched his shoulder.

"Let's join the others," Dr. Frank said. "Lily is out of surgery."

Chapter Ten

"You're a gift from God, Joel." Mia hugged him quickly, too aware of Caleb standing nearby, watching with that disapproving glint in his silver-gray eyes.

"Me?" His eyes, so like Caleb's, stretched wide.

"You. I know God arranged Hilda's surgery to happen at just the right time, while Lily was in the hospital. But now, thanks to you, both of them can recuperate here at Riverbend."

Almost two weeks ago, after visiting Lily, Joel had offered an encouraging word to retired nurse Maisie Smith in the hospital cafeteria after noticing how dispirited she seemed. Maisie told him how she was hoping to find temporary work to provide the funds for her grandson to take a longed-for class trip to Spain. Joel had introduced the nurse to Mia, and the two had soon come to an arrangement.

With a live-in nurse available, Mia had lost

all her reservations about having Lily stay in her home to recuperate. After hearing about Hilda's surgery, she'd invited Lily's caregiver to recuperate at Riverbend, too. Both patients were recovering nicely and everything seemed to be working better than Mia had expected.

"I guess with 'your gift' here, you don't need me hanging around," Caleb muttered in a sour tone. He tossed an affronted look at Joel.

"Of course we need you. Joel's got his hands full with the horses. And I have other plans for you, Caleb." Mia looped her arm through his and smiled at him, relishing the sweet wash of happiness that filled her. After his tender kiss the other day—well, how could he not know she'd always need him?

"What plans?" He looked slightly less disgruntled when Joel excused himself and left.

"You once told me your adopted father, Bud, taught you how to build. Well, a builder is exactly what I need. Or rather, what Lily needs." She described the ramp she wanted outside the back door. "Lily and Hilda will both want to go outside."

"Mia, it's snowing. It's been snowing for days. Even if they did go outside, and that's doubtful given that it's November and freezing cold, there's no place for them to go beyond the back porch." He eased away from her touch.

"I know it's snowing. And I know that right

now going outside is the last thing on their list. But they are going to get bored in here," she said, waving a hand to encompass the house. "They'll want to be outside if only for a breath of fresh air, and I want there to be no barriers. Anyway, Lily is going to have to learn how to navigate through this winter, unless you've found her a home in a tropical climate?"

"I haven't found her a home at all," Caleb said with a wistful edge to his voice. "There just doesn't seem to be anyone willing to take on a child of her age, especially when they learn she's recently had surgery."

"Abby hasn't had any luck, either?" Mia asked. She knew that since Lily's surgery Abby had placed three other children through the Family Ties Adoption Agency. But though she'd contacted all of her former colleagues at child services in Calgary for help, Abby had found no one who would take Lily. Caleb looked so discouraged when he shook his head that she touched his shoulder. "We'll just have to keep praying."

"It hasn't done her any good so far." His face tightened. "Lily's such a great kid. She just wants to love and be loved. Why is that such a hard prayer to answer?"

"Caleb, God isn't going to abandon her." Mia used as firm a voice as she could muster, stuffing down her own questions. "He has plans for that little girl. But in the meantime it's up to us to help her get as mobile as she can, as fast as she can. Hence building a ramp."

"She wants to go to church tomorrow." Caleb grimaced. "I sort of promised she could."

"Caleb!" Mia glared at him. "I know you love her and you can't deny her a thing she asks for, but her surgery wasn't that long ago."

"Dr. Frank said she needs to use the muscles to get her strength back," he defended with a sheepish look.

"Doing the exercises he prescribed. Not by going to church where she'll be bumped and jostled. She might even fall." Exasperated yet understanding that in his desperate love for this child, Caleb was willing to give Lily the moon if it would make her smile. "I'm going to stop praying that you'll adopt Lily." She made herself a cup of tea. "Because I know perfectly well that if God granted my plea and you became her father, that child would be spoiled rotten."

Silence. Mia gulped at the realization that she'd spoken aloud.

"You pray that I'll be Lily's father?" Caleb's voice oozed astonishment. "But—I—"

"Love her," Mia finished. She was so tired of him pretending it was otherwise.

"I can't love her," he insisted. "I can't love anyone."

She whirled on him, fed up with the excuses.

"That's what you tell yourself, isn't it, Caleb?

That you can't love anyone?" She knew from the lines that formed at the corners of his mouth that he was irritated with her, but Mia couldn't stop. "The truth is that you're afraid to love."

"Is that the truth?" His voice emerged tight and clipped.

"Yes, it is," she shot back. "You're afraid to let yourself love because if you did, you might love and lose, just as you lost your mother. And that would hurt. A lot."

"Life hurts." He shrugged and turned away.

"Of course it does. Being alive and open to everything God lets us experience means risking pain. Otherwise we'd be dead." Mia softened her voice, desperate to reach him. "But buried beyond the pain are wonderful memories. Beauty we could not even imagine had we not risked loving."

"Like Bobby?" He faced her then, eyes shooting darts of anger. "Are your memories of him enough to expiate your guilt?"

"Not expiate," she murmured, blanching at the attack. "But was it worth going through what I have to know him?" She nodded. "Yes, a thousand times yes. He came into my life and blessed me. I can never regret loving him—" She choked, unable to say the rest.

Suddenly Caleb was there, wrapping her in his arms and holding her so tenderly. What could she do but lean against this man who'd seen her through the toughest patches of her recent past, despite the cost to himself?

"I'm sorry," he murmured, his lips pressed against her ear. "I'm so sorry, Mia. I shouldn't have said that. I know you loved Bobby, that you only wanted the best for him. What happened was a terrible accident, not your fault."

Mia let herself revel in his words and his touch. His tender embrace was a balm to her battered heart. She wanted so badly to relax against him and just enjoy the moment with this man she loved. But there was more at stake than her happiness here. A terrible weight plagued Caleb and Mia longed to help him break free of it.

"Caleb," she said, not quite certain what she wanted to say because her heart was so full.

"You're wrong about me, Mia. I can't love anyone," he was saying. "I tried so hard to love Lara, but it wasn't there because that part of me shriveled up and died when my father killed my mother. That's why I'll never forgive him." The last words were harsh and bitter; Mia ignored them.

"When Lily was in the hospital, if she needed help what would you have done?" she asked.

"Whatever she needed," he said without hesitation.

"Anything?" she pressed, praying silently for a way to make him see.

"Whatever it took to make her better." He drew back to stare into her eyes, then shook his head as understanding dawned. "That's only natural. Everyone wants to protect a child."

"Do they?" Mia met his gaze and held it, so glad she'd been given the chance to love this wonderful man. "Harlan didn't. Lily was his own flesh and blood, but he felt no compunction to do anything about her injured leg, or her life, or her future. He didn't love her."

"I am not like him," Caleb snapped.

"No, you aren't. Because you love Lily. You want to see her healthy and happy. You want the best for her." She lifted her hand to cup his cheek, mesmerized by the rough, bristly skin that masked a heart as soft as a marshmallow. "That's love, Caleb. That's what love does. 'If you love someone you will be loyal to him no matter what the cost. You will always believe in him, always expect the best of him, and always stand your ground in defending him.'"

"First Corinthians 13," he murmured. His lips brushed her hand as he spoke, sending a sweet shiver of longing straight to her heart.

"Yes." Mia smiled. "You love Lily."

"Yes." Caleb looked stunned yet also thrilled by the admission. "Yes, I do," he said in a firmer voice. He pressed a kiss into Mia's palm. "I love Lily Jones."

"I think you also loved Lara." He opened his mouth to object but she slid her palm from his cheek to his lips and held one finger over them.

"I believe you truly loved her, but your love got blocked out by your anger toward your father."

"Why?" he demanded, easing his mouth away from her touch.

"Because love can't stay where there's hate." It was too hard to stand like this, in the circle of Caleb's arms, and not blurt out her love for him. Mia didn't want to do that, not now. This was the time when he needed to understand what his hate cost him. So she eased away from his embrace but grasped his hand to retain contact. "Your hate pushed out your love for Lara. Are you going to let that keep happening, Caleb?"

Your hate pushed out your love. Are you going to let that keep happening?

The words kept circling inside his head, demanding an answer. Even here among the din of kids whom Joel had brought to Riverbend with their Sunday-school teachers so Lily wouldn't have to miss her beloved church—even now the accusation wouldn't leave him alone.

Hate. Was that how Mia saw him—filled with hate? But that was what he was. Even now as Caleb watched his father sitting with the kids, it churned and boiled inside him. He'd told Mia he wouldn't stay in the house with Joel there, stung when she simply nodded.

Caleb tromped through the snow, moving as far from the house as possible, as if that would help.

Even deep in the woods he couldn't seem to escape the lilting joy in Lily and her friends' voices as they sang "Jesus Loves Me."

"Don't they sound wonderful?"

Caleb should have known Mia would follow him. She seemed to love the snow. But then Mia loved everything and everyone. She wasn't bitter about her past, like him.

"Did you notice how great Joel is with them? He must have been a wonderful dad—" Mia choked off her sentence and risked a look from beneath her lashes. "Before, I mean."

Obviously embarrassed by her faux pas, she silently simply walked with him ever deeper into the woods until there was no sound save the crunch of their footsteps and the odd "puff" as snow fell from heavily laden boughs.

"I've never had a real Christmas tree." Mia, head lifted, was surveying the pines around them. "This year I will have a real tree."

"Not these, I hope." Caleb chuckled when she blinked her surprise. "Mia, they're far too large to fit inside your house. You have to find a clearing where a younger tree is growing."

"And then chop the sweet innocent little tree down?" She scowled. "That sounds horrible."

"It's not as if there's a shortage. You have acres of trees." Caleb couldn't help shouting with laughter at her aggrieved look.

"That's not the point." Tossing him a glare, she

stomped off, then floundered. Caleb reached out and grabbed her arm, hauling her out of the drift.

"Don't step off the path." When her gaze held his Caleb knew she was hinting at a deeper meaning. "To answer your question, my father was a great dad, when he wanted to be. The problem was his drinking started to take more time than his kid."

"He made mistakes," she said. "We all do."

"Most people don't make his 'mistakes.'" Caleb treasured every moment he spent with Mia, loved to listen to her bubbling laughter, to watch her face light up and her emerald eyes dance when she tried to play a trick. She was fun to be with, a pleasure to help and a joy to kiss. But she was fixated on Joel. "Why did you have to hire him?"

"Because I needed help and he is very good at helping." She tilted her head. "Joel is not the father of your childhood, Caleb. He's not the man you remember. He's changed."

"But has he changed enough that he can be trusted around Lily?" Caleb asked.

"Joel would never hurt that little girl, not in a million years, so don't you even imply such a thing." Mia bristled, her eyes like jade chips that flashed with temper. "Lily is desperately lonely and Joel is the closest thing to a grandfather she's ever known. He provides stability and security that she's desperate for."

"*My* father?" He made a face.

"Don't you dare mess with them, Caleb." Mia stomped in front of him and glared. "I will not see that child hurt because you're stuck in the past."

"Adorable Mia. What a mother you are." Caleb couldn't help it. He slid his arms around her waist and hugged her tight, breathing in the scent of pine and snow and sunshine and something indefinably sweet—Mia.

"What are you doing?" She wiggled to get her hands free.

"Hugging you." He tipped his head and pressed his lips to hers. "Kissing you."

She seemed frozen by his kiss. He rubbed his cheek against hers and found it as soft as velvet yet chilly from the winter air.

"Thank you for caring about Lily," he whispered in her ear. "Thank you for being willing to fight for her happiness."

"You're welcome," she managed when she found her voice. A funny look filled her face.

"What are you thinking?" He loved the way she felt in his arms, as if she belonged.

"I was just wondering if you could do that again," she said, her amazing eyes half-hidden by her thick lashes.

Caleb half hoped she meant what he thought she was intimating. But he was afraid to let himself express the feelings building inside him lest he hurt her. He could never tolerate knowing he'd hurt Mia.

To make sure they were thinking along the same lines, he asked, "Do what?"

"Kiss me again. I've never been kissed like that before. I like it," she assured him, twining her arms around his neck.

So did he. Maybe too much. But Caleb's heart swelled inside him as he studied her sweet face. He bent his head and kissed her, slowly and thoroughly, touching her inviting lips with his until she responded and fire built between them. But Mia was an innocent and he didn't want to get her hopes up; despite her assurance, he knew deep inside that he couldn't love her because he hadn't been able to rid himself of his bitterness toward his father. God hadn't answered that prayer.

So after a few moments of pure bliss, he stepped back and let his arms fall away while his head told him he was crazy.

"I don't hear any singing," he said, struggling for composure and avoiding looking at her. "Do you think Sunday school is over?"

"Probably, but they're staying for lunch." Mia slipped her hand into his. "Want to help me make pizza?"

Yeah, he did. In fact, Caleb wanted to help Mia Granger do anything she asked. The only thing he couldn't do was love her. So he walked back to the house, helped her assemble pizzas and reveled in every moment he spent with Mia.

When it was time to eat, the other children

quickly came to the table. Thinking he needed to carry Lily, Caleb was about to enter her room when he heard her speaking. The words made him jerk to a stop and listen.

"Why is Uncle Caleb mad at you?"

"I did something very bad and he can't forgive me." The sorrow in Joel's words struck Caleb in a way nothing his father had said before ever had.

"Did you 'pologize?" Lily asked. "Ms. Hilda says you hafta 'pologize when you do something that hurts somebody."

"I tried, Lily. But I guess some things are too hard to forgive."

"Did you 'pologize to God?" the little girl asked.

"Many times." Caleb could hear the smile in those familiar tones.

"An' He forgave you, right?"

"Yes, He did. In fact, the Bible says after He forgives us, He remembers our sin no more." There was a sound like someone rising from a creaky chair—Mia's old rocking chair. Caleb flinched, needing to move away, but strangely transfixed by the humility and sorrow in his father's words.

"Then, I think Uncle Caleb needs to 'pologize," Lily declared firmly. "We're s'posed to forgive those who trespest against us."

"Trespass," Joel corrected with a chuckle.

"Yeah. I'm going to tell Uncle Caleb that."

"No, Lily. Please don't," Joel begged.

"Why?" Poor Lily sounded confused by his rejection of her help. So was Caleb.

"It's very kind of you, but I'd rather you didn't talk to Caleb about it." His father grunted, a sign he was hefting Lily in his arms. "I don't want Caleb to forgive me because someone asks him to. I want him to forgive me because he wants to."

Silence for a moment. Then Lily said, "Like when Ms. Hilda tells me to 'pologize when that nasty Paul Brown makes fun of my leg but inside I'm still mad at him and I only do it because she makes me?"

"Exactly like that," Joel agreed. "Ready for pizza?"

"Yes."

Joel's chuckle reached out and tugged at Caleb's memories. He stepped into Mia's sewing room so they wouldn't know he'd overheard them. Being surrounded by the myriad colors and textures of Mia's work evoked memories of the many times he'd heard his father's hearty laugh when his mother teased him. Or when Joel had teased her, or Caleb.

When Joel had been sober, they'd been a happy family. Why did he ruin it all?

Why did You let it happen? his heart cried.

A sheet of forest-green fabric sat on Mia's worktable. On it was a piece of paper with words. Caleb leaned closer and read, "Now all that I know is hazy and blurred, but then I will see everything clearly, just as clearly as God sees into my heart right now."

He jerked back, suddenly aware that God saw how his anger and hate had festered, overtaken his thoughts and even his prayer life. He saw how Caleb had resisted every overture his father had made, how he'd refused to give the only thing Joel had asked—forgiveness.

Uncomfortable with the shame that thought brought, Caleb stepped back, prepared to leave the room. His gaze fell on a small quilted plaque that hung above Mia's desk. It held one word. *Forgiven.*

Caleb knew it referred to Bobby. He felt his heart break, knowing the pain she still carried. He was certain that nothing she'd done had harmed that child yet still she, an innocent, sought forgiveness.

Which made Caleb consider how he could see himself as the "forgiver" when there was so much he needed to be "forgiven" for.

"Caleb?" Mia's voice called.

"Coming." He stepped out of her studio with his mind whirling. Yes, he needed to reassess his position with regard to Joel. And he would do that later, when he was alone. But he also had to find out about Bobby. If it would help Mia, he needed to do that.

Caleb felt embittered and angry, locked in his world of hate. But Mia wasn't. After seeing her tender care of Lily, every need met, every question answered, every tear comforted, Caleb was positive sweet, innocent Mia had done nothing to any child for which she needed forgiveness.

Chapter Eleven

"It has to be the best Christmas Lily's ever had." Mia glanced from Caleb to Joel. Both were seated at her breakfast bar with coffee mugs in hand and a plate of cookies in front of them. "And I need you to help me make it so, both of you. Can you manage to work together, for Lily's sake?"

"Of course we can." Joel didn't glance at Caleb. "Where shall we start?"

"With a tree." Conscious of Caleb's silence, Mia dived into her list of things to do. "I want a real tree. So we'll all have to make a trip into the forest to choose it. Joel's arranging a sleigh ride for us?"

"Working on it," he promised.

"Good. We'll cut it down two weeks before Christmas. Now, we'll need to decorate that tree," she continued, smothering her mirth at their groans. "Lily and Hilda and I have already started making some decorations, but I want to take them both to the mall in Calgary to buy more. This is a new house. I'm starting with fresh Christmas traditions. That will include some outside decorations that I'll need help to put up. Okay so far?"

"Take them to Calgary—" Caleb's Adam's apple bobbed up and down as he gulped. "How?"

"We'll rent a van," she said, thrilled with her plan. "Hilda is already managing quite well with her walker. We'll take it along. It has a seat on which she can rest if she needs to. Lily will need her wheelchair. Problems with that?"

Silver eyes stretched wide, the men slowly shook their heads.

"Good." Mia knew neither of them understood why she needed to make this Christmas so special for Lily so she relaxed her tone, desperate to gain their help while they forgot their own problems. "I've been speaking with Lily about Christmas. She's had a dream for years. Her mother never baked cookies with her, didn't have a tree and Lily only ever got one gift. I intend to change all that."

"Can I say something?" Caleb frowned when she nodded. "What happens next Christmas when Lily doesn't have all this—hoopla?" he finally managed.

"She will have it. I will make sure that every Christmas Lily has is special." Mia couldn't tell them she was head over heels in love with Lily or that the child's sweet presence in her life seemed an affirmation of God's love. "This year Christmas will be the special time for Lily that I longed for when I was a child."

"You know that after Christmas, Family Ties will initiate a very strong search for a home for Lily?" Caleb must have seen her shock. "She'll be walking much better by then thanks to your hard work. After the holidays Abby feels Lily's chances will have gone up by leaps and bounds."

Mia gulped, stunned by the thought that she might lose the child she now loved as her own. An idea began to percolate, but she kept it to herself, determined to find out her options before she acted. That was part of managing her own life.

"Lily will love this Christmas." Joel's hand covered hers, transmitting his caring before he let go. "What else can we help with?'

"I want a stack of wood ready for using in the fireplaces over Christmas." Mia paused then clarified, "I'd prefer if we could use only fallen trees or deadwood."

"I can handle that," he promised. "In fact, I'll go get started on it if there's nothing else you need right now."

"Great. Thank you, Joel." She grinned when he finished his coffee, grabbed one last cookie and hurried out the door.

"And me?" Caleb asked.

"I have a very big favor to ask of you." She exhaled then explained. "My house in Calgary is almost complete. I need someone to go through it with me, to make sure the work is as it should be and that nothing's been missed."

"No problem." She loved Caleb's easy acceptance of the job. With him by her side it would be easier to tour the house and not be overcome by the sad memories of the past.

"But that's not all I need." When his eyebrows rose she grinned. "I want to completely decorate the place, down to dish towels and pots and pans, before I hand it over to Arthur. And I want it done so he can move in with his grandkids before Christmas."

"But that's only six weeks away!" Poor Caleb. What a wonderful friend he'd been.

"I know." She reached out and touched his shoulder, needing the contact to remind herself that this man had kissed her passionately and tenderly. He was not aloof and immune. He simply needed to see that giving was a way to heal the heart. "And I have one more even bigger favor."

"Okay." He gulped. "What is it?"

"I need you to go shopping with me." Mia almost laughed as fear filled his silver eyes. He was such a sweetheart.

"Uh, shopping for what?"

"Gifts. For kids." Did his shoulders relax just a bit? "Sixty of them." Nope, he was as tense as before. Mia loved the way he didn't immediately refuse, though he probably wanted to.

"You want to get gifts for s-sixty kids?" Jaw

slackened, Caleb gulped when she nodded. "Where did you get to know sixty kids?"

"They're foster kids I've worked with at my church in Calgary," she explained. "Every year I give them a little something to make their Christmas extraspecial. This year I want to do it again."

"So if you've done it before, why do you need me?" he asked, his curiosity apparent.

"Because the majority of them are boys." She nodded at his understanding. "You see the problem. I'm not up on boy interests, but I'm sure you are. Besides, I think they'd appreciate something other than a quilt."

"You've given all these kids quilts?" Caleb's eyes stretched wide at her nod. "More than one quilt to each?" he asked in a shocked voice.

"No, but I've given them different quilted things. Quilting is what I do." Mia shrugged. "I know it's asking an awful lot of you and that you're busy and probably can't—"

"I'll help you."

"—spare the time, but—what did you say?" She paused, startled. "You'll help me? Really?" At his nod, her smile broke out.

"I'd love to see how that dump of a house came together." He made a face at her frown. "I'm sorry, Mia, but it was a dump."

"I know." She pretended sadness for a moment, but her heart was too light at the thought of spending precious hours in the company of this wonderful man. Maybe he'd even kiss her again. "When?"

"It sounds as if you're a lot busier than me," he said with a grin. "I can reschedule wills, estate planning and real estate sales around your schedule."

"Is that all you do?" She wrinkled her nose. "It sounds boring."

"Thanks." He chuckled when heat burned her cheeks. "No, it's not all I do. The work for Family Ties is the most interesting, but there's not much action right now. Abby has only three women there at the moment and their children have already had adoptions arranged. Not much happens there over Christmas."

"But after Christmas you'll start looking for a permanent home for Lily." Deeply moved by the pain she saw in his face, she asked, "You won't consider adopting her yourself?"

"No." Caleb shook his head firmly. "Lily needs a real home with a mom who's like you, someone who knows how to make her world special. You should adopt her. You could handle it, even with all the other things you've got going on. And you certainly do have a lot."

"My busyness is due to you, Caleb." Mia grinned. "That very first day we met, do you remember what you said?" He shook his head. "You told me I was stronger than I imagined, to consider my opportunities. I took that to heart. God has blessed me beyond measure. I have the resources to help people. In fact, it's my duty. So you see, it's your fault."

"Looks as if I unleashed a lion." Caleb chuckled. "When do we start?"

"Is today too soon? I want to choose the gifts before things get picked over. Besides, they'll need to be wrapped and—" When he held up a hand she stopped. "What?"

"Let's go."

"Thank you. Thank you so much, Caleb." Mia gazed at him, ecstatic at the idea of spending an entire day with him. Then she realized he was looking at her with a question in his eyes. Embarrassed, she hurried to tell Maisie they'd be out and to call Joel if she needed anything. Then she grabbed her jacket and her purse. "I'm ready."

"We'll take my car." When she asked why, Caleb grinned. "Bigger trunk."

"Oh." She smiled back. "Right."

As they drove into the city, Mia couldn't suppress the joy inside. For today she wasn't going to wonder about the future, about what would happen when Caleb finally found a home for Lily and she left or if Caleb would ever return the love she felt for him. Just for today she was going to relax and enjoy every minute she spent with this wonderful man.

* * *

"Are you sure?" Caleb grimaced at clothing Mia had chosen for a boy on her list. "It's not a gift I'd have wanted as a kid."

"You have all your fancy lawyer clothes." She rubbed her finger against his leather sleeve to tease. "Eli doesn't, and the older couple he's living with can't afford to provide the kind of things he needs to attend college classes."

"College? You said he was fifteen?" Caleb appreciated the sheen of her lovely hair cascading around the shoulders of her cream-colored coat.

"He is fifteen and far ahead of kids his age. That's why he's taking college courses." She nodded to the clerk, who suggested several more items. "Please include a gift receipt so he can exchange anything that doesn't suit him," she directed as she handed over her credit card. "Trust me, Caleb. I do know what to get *this* kid. I just never had the opportunity before."

"We can't lug all these bags around. I'll take everything out to the car," Caleb said when the transaction was completed. "Where will you be?"

"In the camera store across the way." She brushed his arm the way she had many times before. And he liked it.

As Caleb walked to the car park, he reflected on how much he liked it that Mia was comfortable with him. Actually there was a lot he liked about his relationship with Mia. For one thing, she continually surprised him. Take these kids; she had tons of information about each child and the family each was with. Those families were included in her gift plans.

"Fostering is hard on others in the house," she'd explained. "A little treat now and then can help ease the adjustment."

That was Mia in a nutshell. Nobody was left out of her generosity. Even the merchants in Buffalo Gap.

"People should support the place where they live," she'd insisted on the ride in. "I've ordered something from almost every store there. What we'll buy in Calgary are things the town's stores don't carry."

Her caring and compassion enriched his growing feelings for her. One of these days Caleb was going to have to figure out exactly how to deal with those feelings, but for today he was going to help where he could and enjoy being with her.

He found her listening to a salesman's spiel about the benefits of buying a camera with six lenses. Mia was clearly overwhelmed by the man's aggressive sales pitch.

"Who is it for?" he asked when Mia glanced at him with a silent plea for help.

"Greg. He's ten, loves photography of every kind."

"Thank you," he said to the salesman. "We'll

think about it." Then he grabbed Mia's hand and steered her out of the store.

"You have a different idea for Greg?" she asked.

"Yes. A simple, easy-to-use camera with the capability to do more once you learn how to use it. You don't want to frustrate his interest with too fancy. Let's try this place." Caleb drew her toward a very small shop where he knew the owner.

Ten minutes later, after Mia paid for the camera she turned and smiled at him. "See, this is why I wanted your help. It's perfect for Greg."

And so it went. Mia told him about the child and his circumstances and Caleb helped her find the place to build those interests. It became a kind of game where he pushed himself to pose different ideas for her to consider. But by noon he was bone tired and starving.

"I need lunch," he said when it seemed Mia could go on forever. "How about here?"

"Chinese?" She bent to study the menu.

"You don't like Chinese food." He stuffed down his sigh and his longing for moo goo gai pan. "A hamburger, then?"

"Oh, I love Chinese food." Mia licked her lips as if to prove it. "I just haven't had it in years."

Since Harlan came on the scene, Caleb guessed.

"Chinese it is." He drew her inside, their packages banging between them. "Why don't you get a table while I go put these in the car? If they'll fit," he muttered only half under his breath.

"Maybe I should have hired that van today." Mia grinned when he looked at her. "We're only half-finished."

"Don't tell me that before I've eaten," he groaned and shuffled out of the restaurant amid her laughter. But as he stuffed her bags into the car, Caleb noted that there was nothing in any of the packages for Mia. Neither had she mentioned wanting any of the many things they'd looked at.

She was going to extreme lengths to make sure everyone she knew had the best Christmas ever. But who would ensure that Mia's Christmas was special? Because of her, many people would find a special gift under the tree. Would she?

As he walked back to the restaurant, Caleb decided to take particular note of her interest in everything. The least he could do was find a gift for her that was something she truly wanted, not flowers or chocolates but something personal that she would remember him by.

And when did Mia remembering you become so important?

That question nagged at Caleb, but he ignored the little voice in his head, Later he'd think about it, he promised himself. Much later.

"Are you sure you want to do this now?" Caleb asked as he pulled up in front of her former home. "You've already had a very full day."

"I want to see what they've done. I want to be

sure they're finished so I can pay off the contractor. He's been great to work with, quick and understanding about my needs. I don't want him to have to wait for his money." Mia inhaled, tossed a smile at Caleb and got out of the car.

"The exterior lights must be on a timer. Good idea." He walked with her to the gate, opened it for her. It neither wobbled nor squeaked. The wrought iron shone dark against the snow, perfectly straight. It gave the house a dignified, cared-for first look.

"Excellent," Mia said, and mentally ticked one item off her list. "The front door's been refinished," she noted as she unlocked it. "Come on in."

She stepped inside, flicked the light switch and stopped, stunned by the beauty of her former home. Behind her she heard Caleb close the door, then he moved to her side.

"I think you'll want to move back here," he said, breaking the silence that had fallen.

"It's amazing. I didn't know opening it up would make it seem so large. That was his idea and I was wary of it because I thought it would reduce the character, but it doesn't. It looks charming." Mia's heart, tight with sad thoughts of returning to this dreary place, now sang. "Arthur and the kids are going to love this."

"The fireplace is gas. Safer and more efficient." Caleb followed her through the living room. "I always knew this staircase would be spectacular," he said in a hushed voice. "It's better than that."

He was right. The stately stairs stood proud and regal in their dark rubbed stain. The treads were covered in a broadloom that would silence footsteps rushing up and down. Mia reached out and sought his hand, needing extra support.

"The kitchen will be the real test," she whispered.

Caleb squeezed her icy fingers in his. "Have faith."

"Yes." She walked forward with him, then gasped. "Caleb, look!"

"I'm looking." He stood beside her, as silent as she, soaking in the details of airy white polished cabinets with moldings and trim wrought by a master hand and finessed by sparkly quartz countertops. A breakfast nook occupied the former sunroom, which had been restored with insulated windows. No longer frigid, the room boasted a tiny fireplace that lent it a cheery feel.

"I could work in here," she whispered.

"Anyone could," Caleb agreed. "Look, French doors to your garden. Want to check out the basement?"

Mia found nothing of the house's former dingy basement. Instead, she saw a huge family room begging for a big television and comfy seating. There was a guest bedroom and a bathroom tucked in the back and a small office to one side that might also be used as a workshop.

"Think your Arthur and his kids will use this?" Caleb asked.

Mia gave him a droll look. She wanted to stay, to let furnishing ideas percolate, but her curiosity was too great. "Let's see upstairs."

Nothing could have prepared her. The master bedroom had huge windows, a squishy soft carpet and an en suite that rivaled the one at Riverbend. The other two rooms shared a Jack-and-Jill bath that was equally luxuriously appointed. Crumbling crown moldings, now repaired and repainted, lent an elegant finish.

"Well?" She turned to Caleb, conscious that, somehow, he still held her hand. She drew it away, embarrassed to be so needy. "Do you see anything that he's missed?"

"Are you kidding? This place could be the center spread in a magazine." Caleb followed her downstairs. "All it needs is furniture."

"Yes." A rush of pleasure zipped through her at the prospect of filling these rooms with beauty. "I can hardly wait." She let the pictures flow through her mind. She could make it so lovely—

"May I say something?" The hesitancy in Caleb's voice and the frown on his face caught her attention.

"What's wrong?"

"Nothing. It's a lovely home. You and the contractor have done a wonderful job," he praised, a soft smile lifting his lips.

"But? I can hear a 'but,' so you might as well say it." Mia didn't know why it irritated her that Caleb couldn't congratulate her and let it go. But she respected him too much to not hear him out.

"I don't want to deflate your bubble." He touched her cheek with his forefinger, smoothing the skin as if to soften what he was about to say. "You should be very proud of this place. It's even more praiseworthy that you want a man and his kids to enjoy it. You are a very amazing woman, Mia. Don't you have even the smallest craving to move back here and enjoy the fruits of your labors?"

"No. This isn't home. My home is at Riverbend Ranch." She tilted her head to one side, reconsidering what he hadn't said. "Do you think I should come back here? Is that what you mean?"

"No," Caleb said firmly. "I just wondered if you had regrets."

"None. So?" He was making her nervous. Caleb had never yet hesitated to speak the truth to her.

"This man, Arthur, and his grandchildren." He chose his words carefully. "Do you think it might be overwhelming for him to move from his apartment to such grandeur?"

Mia gaped at him. She'd never even considered how Arthur and his grandchildren would react, except she'd assumed they'd love this place.

"You want to fill it with beautiful things and I understand that, but maybe they have some of their own cherished possessions that they'd like to bring along. Maybe a bed or a table, something that has good memories." He grimaced. "Maybe I'm way off base."

"No, you're not." Mia managed a smile as her dreams dissipated. "You're exactly right. That's the reason I needed you here. I want this to be a home for Arthur and his family. Not a show home but a place they'll be free to relax, not worry they'll mess up something. Thank you, Caleb."

Mia's heart was so glad he'd risked irritating her rather than let her make a huge mistake that without even thinking she wrapped her arms around his waist and leaned her head on his chest.

"Do you know you're the best friend I've ever had?" she whispered, feeling his heart thud against her cheek. "I love you, Caleb."

Then she stood on tiptoe and pressed her lips against his, trying to show him without words what lay in her heart. His hands came up and gripped her arms and for a moment she thought he would push her away. But a soft groan rumbled somewhere deep inside him and then he was kissing her with a desperation she hadn't expected.

"Oh, Mia," he whispered when at last his lips left hers and pressed to the shell of her ear. "You can't love me."

She tilted her head back to better look at him. "Why not?"

"Because I'm not lovable."

"I think you are. You're kind and generous and concerned about Lily. You go out of your way to help Hilda and you're there whenever Abby needs you for Family Ties. Marsha and Ben can't say enough about the way you've cared for them, made sure they have what they need." She let her fingers trace out the features of his face. "You don't like it but you put up with having Joel around Riverbend because you understand how much I need his help. You care about God and living His way. You're a wonderful man and I do love you, Caleb."

"You shouldn't. You're young and naive. You don't understand the darker side of life. You live in a world of dreams." He stepped back so her arms fell away. "I'm not lovable, Mia. It's no wonder you don't see that. Your goal is to make life better for everyone around you. You make things seem possible but they aren't. I can't love you."

"You don't care about me?" When Caleb didn't answer she stepped closer and spoke as boldly as she dared. "You don't come to Riverbend because you want to see me, to be around me, to laugh with me as I laugh with you?"

"That's not love," he said with a glare.

"Isn't it? Define love for me, Caleb. Tell me what you think it is, because I believe love is sharing good and bad. Love is caring for someone enough to tell him the truth even though you think it will hurt him." She took a breath but refused to stop even though his eyes were getting that frosty look that told her he was annoyed. "Love is holding a little girl while she weeps for her dead mother. Love is agreeing to shop for an entire day and carry packages when you could have ridden with your father up into the hills you love."

She smiled at the surprised look on his face.

"Love is slipping fifty dollars into an old lady's pocket at church because as her lawyer you know she's a little short in paying her heating bill," Mia murmured.

"How did you—?" Caleb stared at her. Then he shook his head. "It wasn't meant to be seen," he muttered.

"Which is also love." Feeling stronger by the moment, Mia smiled at him. "Love is so much bigger than you think, Caleb. You loved your mother, but I believe you love your father, too. In fact, it's not that you don't love Joel. It's that you won't let that love grow. I'm not sure why. Maybe because you see loving him as some kind of betrayal of your mother."

"He killed her!" Caleb said with teeth gritting. "How do you love someone who's done such a thing?"

"You forget about the past and you look at him as God sees us after He's forgiven us, as a new person with nothing from the past to mar us." She slid her hands around his, hoping passionately to finally reach that cold, lonely part of him that couldn't forgive. "You love Joel by giving up the right to be his judge and accepting your role as his son."

Caleb studied her for a long time. Expressions she couldn't understand or define flitted across his face. His eyes softened, lost their ice as he freed one hand to cup her cheek in his palm. Finally he bent and pressed his lips to hers in the most tender kiss Mia had ever received. Tears filled her eyes when he lifted his head and he shook his head.

"I think you are the sweetest, most generous, most kindhearted woman I've ever known, Mia Granger," he murmured. "You shame us all with your generosity of spirit and your bighearted acceptance. I see God in you, in the way you try so hard to extend His love."

"Caleb."

He kissed her silent.

"I wish I could be the man to love you, Mia. To share your amazing world as you bring joy to every life you touch would be a most amazing journey." He kissed her again, then drew away. "But that can't be, because my father would always be between us. To forget what he did to my mother, to dishonor her memory when the only thing she ever did was to love him, to love me—" He shook his head, his eyes brimming with a heartsick sadness. "I wish I could get rid of this lump inside me that demands he pay for what he's done. But I can't. And I won't saddle your life with that."

Mia couldn't say a word. Her heart was breaking and there was nothing she could do about it.

"I'll wait for you in the car. Whenever you're ready," he said quietly.

As she watched him leave, all joy in the day they'd shared, in the house she'd had transformed, all her hopes and dreams dissipated in the knowledge that the only man she'd ever cared about would not be part of her life.

"Am I always to be alone, Lord?" she prayed when the front door closed behind Caleb. "Is love, real love, only for other people?"

Mia let the tears fall, pouring out her heart to the only one who understood. And when her barren soul could weep no more, she brushed away the tears, composed herself and walked out to Caleb's car with one thought uppermost in her mind.

Caleb had said she was strong. Well, she would have to be to survive this longing in her heart. But she'd made up her mind. If she couldn't have his love, she was not going to bury herself in a corner of sadness.

Mia was going to find a way to adopt Lily. She'd ask Caleb to help her. Maybe then he'd understand that love could grow and push out hate and fear and guilt.

Chapter Twelve

"I thought you'd be happy, Caleb." Abby Lebret sat in his office, brow furrowed as she studied him several days later. "Mia wants to adopt Lily. That child could have a wonderful new home with a woman who clearly loves her very much. Why aren't you smiling?"

Because I won't share it with her. Because I'm jealous of a child Mia is showering with love. Because I want to be part of it.

"Surely you don't object to Mia adopting Lily?" Abby's gaze narrowed. "You're her guardian and of course you can object, but why would you?"

"Because *he's* living there." The words seemed to squeeze out of Caleb despite his intent to keep them to himself.

"From what I've seen, Joel is adding immensely to Lily's life." Abby shook her head. "I've done a thorough assessment, Caleb. I've talked to everyone involved and looked at this adoption from every angle. I can't think of anything better than Mia's adoption of Lily, and for Joel to be part of it."

"I thought you'd say that," he admitted.

"It's not just me. I have a hunch that if you tried to stop this adoption and Mia went to court, a judge would see it my way, too. Joel has done nothing wrong," Abby insisted.

"Except kill my mother." Why had he said that? Now Abby, the owner of Family Ties and committed to finding loving homes for needy children, looked at him with pity. Caleb didn't want anyone's pity. Ever.

"How long are you going to drag that around, Caleb?" Abby's dark eyes held sympathy, but her voice remained firm. "This is Lily's chance. Please don't let your issues with your father spoil it. It's time to get over the past."

Why did everyone keep telling him to get over the past, as if he could simply wipe his mother's cruel death out of his mind? *Maybe because Mia did it with Harlan's perfidy?* said an inner voice.

"Not forgiving Joel doesn't hurt him as much as it hurts you." When he didn't respond Abby sighed. "I need to go. Think about what I've said." She rose, handed him her written report, then left.

The intercom buzzed.

"Caleb, Mr. Joel Crane would like to speak to you."

I'll bet he would.

Caleb knew he couldn't put off the confrontation forever, but as tension washed over him, he wanted to refuse to see his father. On the other hand, he wanted to face Joel and demand to know why he was still here in Buffalo Gap. But he was not going to do that in front of his secretary or any of his clients.

"Show him in, please," Caleb said, exerting rigid control as his secretary escorted his father into his office. He did not get up to welcome his guest as he usually did. Instead, he remained seated, jaw tight, waiting until his secretary closed the door behind her.

"Thank you for seeing me, Caleb. I know you're busy." Joel shuffled his feet when Caleb didn't answer, then asked, "May I sit down?"

"If you must." Caleb studied the man he'd despised for so long and noted his father looked old and tired. There was a droop to his shoulders that he'd not noticed before. Gray streaks covered Joel's head, leaving barely any of them the same brown shade as Caleb's.

"I wanted to talk to you about Lily's adoption," his father said quietly.

"I am not at liberty to discuss a client," Caleb informed him in a curt tone. "Is that everything?"

"Is it asking too much for you to just listen?" Joel said. "Please?"

Caleb exhaled, then shrugged.

"Thank you." Joel visibly relaxed. "I know

you're her guardian, Caleb. I also know that you care about her very much. So do I. She's sweet and good, everything you think I'm not. I couldn't love her more if she were my own grandchild. I think Lily loves me, too."

"You don't deserve to be loved," Caleb said bluntly.

"None of us deserve that."

The words reminded Caleb of Mia and her comment long ago that no one "deserved" God's love. Joel seemed to read his mind.

"It's by God's grace that I live and breathe. I know that." He leaned forward. "I didn't kill your mother, Caleb. I know you think you saw me do that, but that is not what happened."

"I've heard all this—" Caleb began, but his father interrupted his brush-off.

"I was drunk, yes. I was angry, yes. In fact, I was in a rage. Booze did that to me. Most of the time I blacked out, but I didn't that day. I was arguing with your mother and I saw her step back. I reached out to grab her, to save her, but she backed away. And she fell." Tears coursed down Joel's cheeks, but Caleb ignored them.

"That's your story?' he said in his most scathing voice.

"That's the truth," Joel insisted. "I didn't push her, but in a way I did cause her death. She wouldn't have fallen if we hadn't been arguing. Nothing can change that. I will bear it on my conscience for the rest of my life. But I did not push your mother."

"What does any of this have to do with Lily?" Caleb said when the silence stretched too long.

"I love Lily. I want that precious little girl to have a home where she is loved. She loves you, Caleb. She believes you will do the right thing for her. I believe you will, too," Joel said, his gaze intense as it held Caleb's. "So let me help you help her."

Caleb's radar went up. What was his father after?

"If having me in Lily's life is a barrier to you allowing Mia to adopt her, I will leave Riverbend and Buffalo Gap. I will not allow anyone else to suffer because of my actions." Joel rose. Funny how he looked so dignified now, shoulders back, eyes clear, body poised.

On the other side of his massive desk, Caleb felt small.

"If that's what holds you back from approving Mia's adoption of Lily, say the word and I'll be gone."

"Really? You'd leave, just like that?" Caleb didn't believe it.

"Just like that. I love that little girl as much as I once loved you, still love you," Joel said, meeting his gaze with a clear stare. "That's why I will not do anything to hinder her future."

"What about your vow that you wouldn't leave

until what's between us is settled?" Caleb asked. Why did he feel that he'd lost the advantage here?

"I'll leave that to God. I can't do any more." Joel turned to leave, paused, then turned back. "I'm sorry I ruined your life, Caleb. I'm so sorry you lost your mother, your home, your life. But now you've been given a precious gift. Mia loves you. Don't throw that away because of our past, because of me."

There were a thousand things Caleb wanted to throw at him. And yet hadn't there been enough words?

"Let me know," Joel murmured, his eyes wet. "It won't take me long to pack." He quietly slipped out of the room.

And Caleb, who was used to being in control in his own office, knew he'd won his case but lost the most important battle of his life.

"I know you've been avoiding me." Three days later Mia stood, hands on her hips and she glared at Caleb. She'd bearded him in his office out of concern for Lily. At least that was what she told herself. "You can avoid me all you want, but there's a little girl who desperately misses you and I'm done making excuses for your absence. Go see Lily."

She turned and stalked to the door. But before she could grab the doorknob he spoke.

"I have been avoiding you. And it's been awful.

Can we be friends again?" Caleb's amazing eyes twinkled, sending her heart rate into the stratosphere.

"What does being friends mean?" she asked cautiously, afraid to trust his words when he'd told her he couldn't love her.

"It means helping you get this Christmas extravaganza you're planning under way. Deal?" He held out his hand.

"Okay." Mia slipped her hand into his for a moment, then drew back. She'd exposed her heart and he'd rebuffed her. That hurt far worse than anything Harlan had done. She would not allow herself to be that vulnerable again. Caleb had been right. She was strong. She had to handle being around him without letting herself dream he was offering anything other than friendship.

"Thank you," he said quietly.

"You're a bit late getting on board." Mia loved the way he looked at her, as if she were more than just a friend. "We've already done a lot, but there's still the trip to the mall for Lily and Hilda."

"Monday? I haven't much on my schedule that day, so it's easily cleared. The crowds won't be so bad then, either. I'm pretty sure I can arrange a van rental in time." He lifted one eyebrow, waiting for her decision.

"Fortunately Lily's still doing her schoolwork at home, so yes, that works. Then we'll need to get a tree. Joel's rebuilt an old-fashioned sleigh so we can take Lily and Hilda for a ride to choose the right one."

"How's she doing?" he asked softly. Mia knew he meant Lily and not Hilda.

"Very well, according to her physiotherapist. It helps that she has a solo with the kids' choral group for the Sunday-school program they're performing on Christmas Eve. Lily insists she's going to walk onto the platform unaided. Joel built her an apparatus to help her manipulate stairs."

"Good." Caleb nodded. Mia's breath caught in her throat at his intense gaze.

"I'm afraid she's pushing too hard, but her physiotherapist says to let her work as hard as she wants." She was babbling and she knew it, but her mind was replaying his kiss and every part of her wanted to repeat that experience. "Joel and Hilda and I each keep a close eye on her."

"You haven't had your cookie-making session yet, have you?" Caleb looked so disappointed when she nodded that Mia made a snap decision.

"We'll need to have another, though. I'm going to throw a Christmas party at Riverbend after the Sunday-school concert. I'll invite anyone who wants to come." As she said it, Mia felt a rush of satisfaction. A party was exactly what everyone under her roof needed.

"Count me in for the baking day," he said.

"Okay, but before that I need to get my Christmas lights put up outside. I was planning to get some in Calgary, but the hardware store here had such a wonderful supply that I just bought a ton." She glanced at him sideways. "Joel and I are going to put some of them up tonight, I hope. I want the ones that hang from the eaves to go up first."

"You're not going up a ladder to hang Christmas lights, Mia," Caleb said, just as she'd hoped he would. "If you feed me dinner, I'll help hang the lights."

"With Joel?" she asked, studying him.

Caleb slowly nodded. "If he has to be there."

"He does. Thank you. I'll appreciate your help. Now I'd better get home and start preparing dinner." She turned to leave. Caleb's hand on her arm stopped her.

"I spoke to Dr. Frank this morning, Mia. He told you Lily's recovery is a little slower than he'd expected?" He waited for her nod. "What if she doesn't get complete mobility? What do we do then?"

"Where's your faith, Caleb?" Mia heard the sharpness in her voice and modulated it. He was only speaking her fears. "Whatever happens, Lily will still be Lily and I will always want to adopt her. Is that what you're asking?"

"Not exactly, but thank you for clarifying." He shook his head.

"What?"

"That faith of yours, doesn't it ever weaken?" he asked.

If only he knew how hard it was to keep trusting God to work things out, to keep believing that He'd given her this deep love for Caleb for a reason.

"It's taken a hit lately," she said, holding his gaze with hers until she knew he caught her meaning. Summoning the faith he'd praised, she quoted, "'I know the plans I have for you, plans to prosper you and not to harm you.' God knows what He's doing, Caleb. Remember that." She waggled her fingers at him in a wave. "See you later."

As Mia drove the snow-covered road home, she recalled a sermon she'd heard long ago.

From time to time it's good to review the past so we can see what God has done, how He's worked things out in ways we could never imagine.

Mia thought of Harlan and the life of deceit she'd endured at his hands. That had ultimately led her here to Buffalo Gap, where she'd found joy and a child to love. That move had also given her the opportunity to make the house where she'd endured loneliness into a place of joy for Arthur and his kids.

Because of Caleb, Mia had not filled it with all the lovely furniture she'd imagined. Instead, she'd consulted Arthur about what he'd prefer and together they'd bought only a few serviceable pieces because he'd chosen to bring many of his own possessions. Some were damaged, but he'd insisted he could fix them. At first dubious, after her visit with him yesterday Mia realized those old things were what made the house exactly what she'd wanted—a home where old memories could be built on. Her former house was now a place where love prevailed.

"You worked it all out," she murmured, turning into her driveway and pulling into her garage. "So I'm trusting You with Caleb, too. Please work on his heart, work out his issues with Joel. And help Lily and Hilda recover fully. Please let this Christmas be a truly joy-filled one, for all of us."

It was up to God now. All she had to do was trust Him to soften Caleb's hardened heart so love could fill his life. Her love.

"I've eaten so much I don't know if I can climb up the ladder again," Joel said, pushing away from the table.

"Again?" Caleb frowned. Though it had almost melted now, sleet had pelted the valley earlier. He'd had to use his four-wheel drive to get to Riverbend. He couldn't imagine climbing a ladder outside in such weather.

"I hooked the clips on the eaves troughs to hang the lights. I thought that would be easier in daylight." Joel met his gaze without rancor, then thanked Mia for the meal. As he hugged Lily good-night, Caleb watched his father's eyes close and saw the look of pure bliss fill his face. "Sweet dreams, sweet one," Joel whispered.

"Good night, Pops." Lily clung to his hand for a minute, letting go only after he kissed her cheek. Pops? When had that happened?

"I'm going to do the dishes," Hilda announced. "Without help," she insisted, shooting Mia a look that said *don't argue with me*. "I'm looking forward to seeing those lights up when I come back from prayer meeting tomorrow night."

"Our cue to get to work." Caleb rose, carried his dishes to the counter by the sink, then walked to the front door to don his coat, boots and gloves. To his surprise, Mia dressed to go outside, too.

"You didn't think I'd let you do this on your own, did you?" she teased. "I have a plan."

"Of course you do." With her masses of hair bound inside a knitted green cap that matched her eyes, Caleb thought she looked adorable. A matching scarf around her neck was tucked inside her cream jacket. On her hands she wore bright red mittens. "You look like a goofy Christmas elf," he teased as he tucked an escaping tendril of hair behind her ear.

"You may pay for that later," she warned with a grin, then went outside.

Caleb had dreaded this time of working with Joel. He'd only agreed because he knew how much Mia wanted to make her long-cherished Christmas dream come true. But in actuality, it was fun to hang the gazillion icicle lights.

"Did you buy out the store?" he asked when the

strands were finally hung and sparkled their soft white glow into the night.

"Pretty much." She winked at him. "I had to. I have a big house."

"Understatement," Joel muttered with a sideways grin at Caleb. "What's next?"

"Lights on some of these gorgeous spruce trees," Mia said cheerfully.

Caleb insisted on being the ladder man. But the trees were huge. Even the extension ladder wasn't long enough to reach the top. It took some persuasion for Mia to agree to decorate the shorter ones. She reiterated her dream of lighting the large trees.

"Say, I met a fellow in town with a ladder truck who was decorating that big tree in the town square," Joel remembered when they'd finished decorating five smaller spruce trees. "Maybe you could hire him to string lights on your larger trees on either side of the house."

"Don't encourage her," Caleb begged, descending from the fifth and final tree. A second later he felt the cold, wet smack of a snowball against his neck. "Hey!"

"This is where I say good-night," Joel said, and quickly strode across the snow toward his bunkhouse.

"Good night, Joel. Thank yo—ach!" Mia spat out the mouthful of snow and glared at Caleb. "I warned you," she said before hurling a snow missile with incredible accuracy and speed. It caught him squarely on the forehead.

"Okay, I give. I give," he yelled after Mia had targeted him several more times. He dodged more missiles and finally threw up his hands. "You win."

"Yes, I do." She approached him, grinning from ear to ear. "Just call me the queen of snowball fights. Let's build a snowman."

Caleb was chilled and ready to go inside, but he just couldn't deny her the simple pleasure. He would have slapped the thing together just to get it done, but Mia had precise expectations and produced a kitchen knife to make the snow creature fully rounded from all aspects.

"Good enough?" he asked, sure there was not an edge left anywhere.

"Almost." Mia pulled a soft black hat out of her pocket and perched it on the snowman's head. She added a carrot nose and something dark for snowman eyes. Finally she took her green scarf and wrapped it around his neck. Then she stood back and surveyed their work, her breath mingling with his. She linked her arm through his and tilted her head to the right so it rested on his shoulder. "Perfect. You build a good snowman for a lawyer, Caleb."

Somehow Caleb couldn't stop himself from sliding his arm around her waist and drawing her against his side.

"Teamwork," he said, now perfectly content to stand in the cold and stare at the light show he'd created with this most amazing woman.

"Look up," she whispered.

He did and saw Lily watching them. He waved and she waved back. Then her bedroom light went out.

"Minx. She's supposed to be asleep." Mia chuckled. "You probably woke her up when you bellowed over getting a little snow in your face."

"Probably." He knew what she was doing. She was keeping things light to avoid the intimacy they'd shared when they were last together. Part of Caleb was relieved, but part of him wanted to throw caution to the wind, pull her into his arms and kiss her until she asked him to stop. Part of him wanted to look forward to a host of Christmases to come.

"Tomorrow I'm going to build a fort," Mia said. "Lily wants one."

"And what Lily wants, Lily gets. You're going to be a doting mother," he said, surprised by how saying those words brought sweet delight to his heart.

Mia twisted to look at him, her face mere inches from his.

"Am I going to be Lily's mother, Caleb?" she asked in that breathy tone that told him she was thrilled by the prospect but afraid to let her hopes get too high. He guessed she'd feared he'd use

Bobby's death against her. Because she didn't trust him.

"I think you're made for each other," he said so quietly she had to lean near to hear.

"Oh, Caleb, thank you." In a flash she curled her arms around his waist, stood on tiptoe and pressed her lips to his. A second later, much too soon for his taste, her kiss ended. "Thank you so much. I promise I will always love her."

"That's why Lily belongs with you." Her face shone with joy in the glow of the Christmas lights. No matter where he went in the future, Caleb knew he'd always remember the deep rich green of her eyes, the smooth curve of her cheek and the tendrils of hair that had escaped her cap and now framed her lovely face.

"I'm not sure about a lot of things," he admitted. "But I know with certainty that God brought the two of you together. No one could take better care of her, love her more deeply or work harder to make her happy. You *are* her mother."

"Oh, Caleb." Her sweet voice caressed his soul while her eyes begged him for—something. The temptation was too great.

Caleb bent his head and covered her lips with his, loving the tiny shiver Mia gave but knowing that taking the love she so freely offered was wrong. He would only hurt her again.

Slowly, gently, he broke off their kiss and

stepped back, repressing the urge to reach out and stop her arms from leaving his waist.

"Hot chocolate?" she whispered, her voice slightly hoarse.

"I better go home." He couldn't stop himself from trailing a finger down her velvety cheek. "Thank you for a wonderful evening, Mia."

"Come again," she invited, her lips curving in a sweet smile.

He would. That was the problem. Caleb couldn't stop coming back to Riverbend, even though he knew he'd run into his father, even though he knew he'd have to struggle to resist kissing Mia.

But that wasn't love. It couldn't be, because love didn't intentionally hurt, and despite knowing how much both Mia and Lily cared for him, Caleb had every intention of asking Joel to leave Riverbend and Buffalo Gap. It was the only way he could expiate his need to avenge his mother's death.

But for Mia's sake he would wait until after Christmas.

Chapter Thirteen

"I thought you'd never get here, Uncle Caleb." Lily gave him a dark look. "Christmas is only seventeen days away."

"I'm sorry, sweetheart." He smoothed the dark hair and pressed a kiss to her forehead. Mia thought that was to avoid her condemning look. "I got busy."

"Too busy." Lily's dark blue eyes filled with reproach.

"Uncle Caleb is here now and Joel has the sleigh outside, so let's go get that tree." Mia avoided Caleb's glance, a little shy around him after his intense kiss by the snowman a week ago. She felt confused, at odds. One minute he was kissing her; the next she didn't see him for ages. What was going on?

There was no time to dwell on Caleb's odd behavior as she handed him a thermos of hot cocoa, a plastic container with treats and blankets to cover Lily and Hilda. Joel had cleared a wide path from the house. With him on one side and Caleb on the other, Lily and Hilda walked slowly over the path to the sleigh and with both men's help, sat on the backseat. Mia would have joined them, but Caleb insisted she sit up front between him and Joel.

As a buffer? she wondered. But since both men were working hard to avoid all contentious issues, she didn't ask.

"Isn't it fun, Mia? I never had a sleigh ride before." Lily chatted nonstop, clearly excited. She pestered Caleb by asking constantly if the tree they were passing was their Christmas tree. At first he tried to explain, then simply shook his head no.

"Wait, sweetie," Joel urged her. "We'll come to the best ones pretty soon."

Lily launched into her Christmas solo and then they all joined her in a round of Christmas carols. By then they were deep into the woods.

"Just a bit farther," Joel said almost under his breath.

"You've been out here before?" Caleb asked with a frown.

"I had to make sure it was okay for the sleigh," Joel said. "But I've walked almost every inch of Riverbend."

"Why?" Caleb demanded.

"Thinking, praying. Enjoying God's creation.

Now, Lily, what do you think?" He drew the two horses Mia had inherited to a halt and smiled as Lily, wide-eyed and finally silent, gazed around the clearing. "See any Christmas trees you like?"

"All of them." Lily pointed left then right, her excitement growing. Mia touched her arm.

"Take a good look, honey, because we need exactly the right tree for our Christmas. Okay?" She smiled when Lily nodded.

Joel drove them around the clearing, turning this way and that so they could see the trees from every angle. Finally Lily pointed.

"That one. Right, Mia?"

Mia nodded, unable to speak because of the joy she found in this moment.

"I'll come back tomorrow and cut it down," Joel promised. "While you're at the mall in Calgary."

"And next summer we'll come back here and plant a new one to take its place." What would next year bring? she wondered. Would Caleb have forgiven his father by then? Would Lily be able to run through the meadow among the trees?

Would God have answered her plea for Caleb to love her?

Thrusting away the doubt that bubbled inside, Mia asked if Joel could park the sleigh near their chosen tree.

"I think we should have a winter campfire," she said.

"I've never done that before." Lily's eyes grew

huge when Caleb lifted her from the sleigh. "What if I fall, Uncle Caleb?" she said, her fear evident.

"Then, you'll get up." He chucked her cheek. "That's what we all do, darlin'."

Mia saw Joel glance at him, saw Caleb's expression tighten.

"If you men will build the fire, I have hot chocolate and some treats we can enjoy." She glanced at Hilda. "There's a bare spot under the massive pine tree. It might be a good place to collect those pinecones you wanted."

"It certainly is." Hilda pushed forward in the sleigh and held out a hand. "Joel, would you mind helping out an old woman?"

Joel almost sprinted forward to offer his hand. Mia blinked, astonished by the sweet glance that passed between the two. She hadn't given a thought to Joel and Hilda building a relationship, but it was obvious as he escorted her across the snow and helped gather the acorns she wanted that they'd grown very fond of each other.

"That's your doing?" Caleb's mouth tightened into a grim line.

"Me?" Mia shook her head. "I had no idea. But I'm very happy for both of them."

"Nothing can come of it." He glared at her. "He's not to be trusted. I need to tell Ms. Hilda that."

Furious that he would allow his grudge against his father to ruin the happiness these two obviously might find together, Mia let her anger spill out.

"Are you so selfish that you can't allow anyone to be happy, Caleb?" She kept her voice low so Lily, who was making snow angels a few feet away, wouldn't hear. "Will that make your mother's death more palatable? Would she have approved of this vendetta you seem determined to carry out?"

Mia stomped away to join Lily. With that child's joy in life, goofy jokes and unstoppable laughter, Mia's anger quickly dissolved. She let Caleb build the fire, and when Hilda and Joel returned with their stash of pinecones, she spread out her picnic and poured a cup of hot chocolate for everyone. Though she sensed Caleb's glance, she refused to meet it. But her heart ached.

If only...

"'My help comes from the Lord,'" she reminded her sagging spirit.

The sleigh ride home was a lively affair. Hilda told them of her plans to use pinecones to make old-fashioned wreaths to decorate Riverbend. Lily fussed over what to wear for her solo performance while Joel pointed out chickadees, partridges, a snowy owl and a spruce grouse that flapped its wings angrily before moving out of their path.

Mia smiled and pretended nothing had changed, but for her the joy had gone out of the excursion. Caleb, too, seemed introspective. Joel disappeared with the sleigh after helping Lily and Hilda inside. By the time Caleb had brought in some wood for the fireplace Lily wanted lit, Joel had returned, the chosen Christmas tree in the back of the sleigh.

"Can we decorate it tonight?" Lily begged as she danced around Caleb and Joel, who had finally managed to get the tree inside the house and into its stand.

"Not tonight," Mia said, hating the disappointment that filled Lily's face. "The branches must warm up because they'll droop a little and we'll need to trim it."

"That's where the term 'trim the tree' came from," Hilda explained.

"Tomorrow?" Lily pleaded.

"Maybe, if we're not too tired when we get back from Calgary," Mia temporized, worried Lily might push herself too hard after a day at the mall. "We have to pick out your Christmas dress, remember?"

"Oh, yeah." Lily's face brightened. She turned to Caleb. "You're coming with us, too, right, Uncle Caleb?"

"I'm afraid I have to cancel. I've taken on a new case and I have a lot of preparation," he said to Mia over Lily's protests.

"On Sunday?" she murmured, arching one eyebrow, suspicious that he was simply trying to get out of his promise.

"Yes, because my client has been ordered to

make a court appearance tomorrow morning," Caleb said softly. "I'm sorry, but—"

"You can't make the trip to Calgary," Mia finished, surprised by the rush of disappointment welling up inside. They'd had such a wonderful time on their last visit to the city.

"I really am sorry," Caleb said in a soft voice when Lily had wandered away grumbling.

Mia nodded as she struggled not to show how let down she felt. "I'll handle it."

"On your own?" His frown did nothing to mar his handsome good looks.

"I'm strong, Caleb. Remember?" she said to remind him of his own words. She shrugged. "Joel will come with us. We'll be fine."

"I do worry about you, Mia." His silver eyes met hers directly. She thought she saw a hint of softness there, but a second later it was gone and his tone was all business. "The van will be here with the driver at nine. He'll drive you to and from Calgary and anywhere else you want to go."

"Thank you." There seemed little more to say. Apparently Caleb realized it, too, because a moment later he was driving away from Riverbend while a hole opened up inside Mia's heart.

"Father?" she whispered helplessly.

Whence comes my help? My help comes from the Lord.

"This is my lesson on trust, isn't it?" she said,

staring into the twilight outside, watching Caleb's taillights disappear. "Keep me strong, Lord."

Caleb deliberately did not visit Riverbend in the days following Mia's Calgary trip. Oh, he called several times during the week, just to make sure everything had gone well, that Hilda and Lily were no worse for wear. But mostly he called simply to hear Mia's voice.

"We're fine, Caleb. Preparing for Christmas. In fact, we're baking cookies this afternoon if you want to join us."

Did her careful, polite tone hold just a hint of longing? For him? She'd said she loved him. Did she still, or had she given up on him?

"Never mind," Mia said when he didn't answer. "I know you're busy. You can taste the fruits of our labors whenever you're able to stop by. Just call first in case I've taken Lily to practice her solo. You haven't forgotten the Christmas program Sunday night, have you? Or my party after?"

He hadn't forgotten. How could he? Everything about Mia was implanted on his brain: the way her hair curled and waved around her lovely face; the way she smiled, wholeheartedly, unabashedly inviting the world to join her; the wide-ranging plans she devised to bring as much joy to those around her as she could manage.

No, he hadn't forgotten anything about Mia Granger, though he'd tried to.

"Caleb?" Her gentle voice brought him back to the present. "I'm sorry. I'm prattling on and disturbing your busy day, aren't I? I'll let you go. Feel welcome to join us anytime." She hung up before he could tell her he would never be too busy for her.

Caleb avoided visiting Mia because seeing her and not holding her, not kissing her was too hard. He knew he would only hurt her. The desperate hunger in his soul to be part of her life had finally sent him to his knees, to beg God to take away the anger and misery his father's presence had brought. He'd prayed hard and long to be free of the past, yet the cold, hard lump of unforgiveness still sat in his stomach like a lead-weight reminder of all he'd lost.

Seeing Mia, being with her, watching her joy in life fill her lovely face only made Caleb realize anew that she was all the things he wanted. She made his life worthwhile. She made him a better man. But after hearing her voice today, Caleb finally accepted that for all his daydreams about a future with Mia, he would never enjoy sweet, precious moments with her again unless he could find a way to let go of the past and reconcile with his father.

"But how, God?" he said as the familiar rush of bitterness rose inside. "He doesn't deserve forgiveness."

He had to find a way, because Caleb suddenly

realized that the law he loved was no longer enough to fill his heart. Mia did that.

Because he loved her? Yes, his heart screamed. He loved Mia. She made his world interesting, fun and worthwhile. He couldn't imagine a world where he couldn't see her, where he couldn't be near her to share her worries and her joys. This soul-deep yearning to share every one of Mia's tomorrows with Lily no matter what happened *had* to be love.

For a moment he dreamed it was possible.

Then Joel's face filled his mind. Joel embracing Lily. Joel sharing a smile with Mia. Joel and Hilda. In an instant indignation shoved out his love for Mia. What could he possibly offer her with this lump of forgiveness lodged in his throat? Nothing.

Except maybe some freedom from the past.

For a long time Caleb sat in his empty office alone. Then he got to work on a very special Christmas gift for Mia.

Chapter Fourteen

Mia sat in the darkness of the church sanctuary, heart in her mouth, as Lily hobbled unsteadily onto the stage. Glossy dark ringlets bobbed as she smoothed the skirt of her blue velvet dress and rearranged the lace. Then she lifted her gaze to the audience.

Fear darkened the little girl's deep blue eyes. Mia's heart squeezed with love. She could go up and rescue her, but Lily had practiced and anticipated her achievement for so long. Mia desperately wanted her to achieve her goal.

Help her, she prayed silently.

A rustle beside her drew her attention. Caleb. He was looking straight at Lily. He smiled and nodded, then sat down beside Mia.

"I hope you don't mind if I join you."

Mia shook her head but couldn't say a word. Sitting next to Caleb, his shoulder rubbing hers— why would she object to that? Feeling guilty for the rush of happiness suffusing her while Lily suffered, she returned her gaze to the stage and stared.

Lily was smiling. She nodded once to the pianist and the music began. Her voice soared, sweetly announcing the birth of a baby who would save the world. Every note sounded perfect to Mia. She was spellbound by the joy radiating from Lily as her voice glided and dipped, strong and forceful, then soft as a whisper. As the last notes died away, Mia felt a tear trickle down her cheek. After a moment of pure silence, the church erupted in applause. As Lily walked regally from the stage, Mia was certain no one noticed her leg brace.

"She did it." Caleb grabbed her hand and squeezed it. "She was perfect, wasn't she?"

Mia nodded. With his beloved face mere inches away, the longing to touch him was overwhelming. But Caleb had made it clear that he could not love her.

As the music concert continued, with her heart breaking, Mia finally and completely turned Caleb and her love over to God. It wouldn't be easy. She still loved him desperately, trusted him and yearned to share a future with him. But Mia finally accepted that only by placing her total trust in God could she face life without Caleb.

When the concert was over and Pastor Don had praised everyone for their efforts, he reminded the congregation of Mia's invitation to her Christmas party. While Caleb spoke to friends, Mia collected Lily, Hilda and Joel and drove home, assuring Lily that her solo had been perfect while her heart begged God for comfort.

Caleb stood in the shadows of the sanctuary, listening to Mia repeat her assurance to Lily that she'd done a good job. He didn't need anyone to tell him; he could see how much the two loved each other in the way they looked at each other, touched each other. It was also evident that both Lily and Mia cared for his father. They easily included him in their group, smiling and laughing.

Envious of that love, Caleb let himself imagine he could be part of their world. But not with Joel, never with Joel. He walked out of the church, bitterness simmering inside him. Why did his father always have to spoil it?

"Honey?" Marsha dragged on his arm, stopping him from getting to his truck. "You're going to Mia's party, right?"

"I'm not sure." He hesitated. How could he go there, watch his father enjoy himself and not say something? That would ruin the party Mia had worked so hard to make. "I'm kind of—"

"Busy?" she demanded, one eyebrow arched. "Did it ever occur to you that you're too busy, Caleb? One of these days you're going to look back and realize that because you didn't grab the opportunity, you've missed the joy and love that God created especially for you."

"Marsha—"

"You listen to me, Caleb," she interrupted. Her voice had that stern tone that told him he was in trouble. "I'm your mother in every way that counts, so I'm going to tell you the cold hard truth."

"You always do," he said, trying to defuse her speech by making a joke. Marsha was not amused.

"Mia loves you. She doesn't care about your past or that bitterness you hang on to like a security blanket. Mia only wants you to be happy. That's real love, and it doesn't come around that often." She tilted her head. "But you know that, don't you, Caleb? Because you love her."

"It wouldn't work," he said, wishing she'd let it alone.

"You're God now? You know these things?" Her fierce glare pinned him. "Lara loved you and you tried to love her back but couldn't."

"I can't love anyone." Even to himself his words sounded silly.

"You don't love me? You don't love Bud?" Her scathing glower told him she knew differently.

Driven by her attack, Caleb did away with the niceties.

"I can't be around Mia when he's there. I can't stop the loathing and disgust I feel," he admitted.

"So? When I see chocolate, I can't stop wanting it. Does that mean I have to act on that feeling?" Marsha suddenly enveloped him in her arms and hugged tight. "I love you, Caleb," she said in a broken voice. "You're a good man who truly cares about helping people. You've achieved so much. But that sad little boy inside won't let you be free. He's keeping you from loving a woman who could enrich your life."

"Mom—"

"Let go of the past, Caleb. Please, before it drags you so far down you'll miss every wonderful thing God has for you." Marsha kissed his cheek, gave him one last hug and then, after a searching look, walked toward her husband.

As they drove away, Caleb knew he would go to Mia's party. He'd only been fooling himself that he could stay away from her.

For Mia's sake he would hold his tongue and endure his father's presence. But after the party he would seek Joel out and ask him to leave, as he'd promised. Maybe then Caleb could finally break free of his past.

Mia reveled in her teeming home, loving the sound of laughter as people mingled together. This was what she'd dreamed of when she'd first moved to Riverbend. But her dreams had grown and changed. Soon Lily would be her daughter in word and deed. But Caleb would never—

"Looks as if everyone's enjoying themselves."

The object of Mia's thoughts suddenly appeared in front of her. "You've done a great job with the decorations and the food." Caleb held up a gingerbread man she and Lily had made. "I like the buttons best."

"Most kids do like chocolate," she teased.

"The tree looks stunning." His eyes glowed soft and warm. "I don't think all those stars came from the local store."

"Actually Hilda and Joel made them." She noted his wince at the mention of his father. "Excuse me. Some folks are leaving. I need to say goodbye, but please don't go. I want to ask you a favor."

Mia's hostess duties kept her busy for a half hour. By the time she saw Caleb again, her guests were gone. Joel and Hilda were cleaning up the kitchen with Lily when Caleb found her staring into the glowing embers in the fireplace.

"I think it's time for me to head out, also," he said.

"I'm glad you came." Mia couldn't stop staring into his eyes, wishing for the impossible. "I wanted to ask if you could drop Lily off at the Pembertons' in town. She's going for a sleepover. Ashley has the measles and according to her mom needs serious diversion."

"Which Lily can provide because she's already had them." He nodded and wrinkled his nose. "I remember that occasion vividly. She tested all of our patience."

"That's why the Pembertons want her to come distract Ashley. I'd take her, but I'm really scared to drive on these icy roads after dark, though everyone else around here seems to take it in stride."

"We're used to it." He shrugged.

"Yes, well, maybe by next year I will be, too. Anyway, I hoped you could take Lily and save me disappointing her." Mia grinned. "She'll keep you entertained on the way. You know Lily. Always full of ideas."

"Believe me, I know. Sure, I'll drop her off." He looked at her, stared really. Mia's cheeks grew warm.

"Uncle Caleb, come get your goody bag," Lily called from the doorway. "I made it for you."

"Thank you, sweetheart." Mia walked with him, watched as Caleb took the bag and peeked inside. "Chocolate-chip cookies. Thank you."

"Welcome. Mia helped me. And Ms. Hilda. And Pops." Lily giggled when Joel appeared and tickled her under the chin.

Mia's heart broke as joy drained from Caleb's face.

"Go get your coat, Lily. Uncle Caleb is going to drop you off at Ashley's for the sleepover," Mia said quietly.

"Goody. I already got my backpack in the closet." Lily moved, stopped, then grinned. "You gotta kiss Mia, Uncle Caleb."

"What? Why?" Caleb looked as if he found the prospect distasteful.

"'Cause you're standing under the mistletoe. Me an' Pops put it there." Lily's smile never wavered. Her eyes sparkled with mischief, moving from Caleb to Mia, apparently oblivious to the tension in the room. "Kiss her, Uncle Caleb."

With no choice, Caleb bent his head and pressed his lips against Mia's. Though it wasn't the most romantic kiss they'd ever shared, the touch of his lips on hers brought back the hopes and dreams Mia had tried so hard to quash. She kissed him back, hoping he'd understand how much she loved him, how much she wished he would kiss her for the rest of his life.

But Caleb drew away.

"We need to get going." His voice was hoarse. "Mia will help you to my car. I need to talk to Joel for a moment. Alone."

The sharpness of that last word, the intensity in Caleb's eyes and the way he glared at his father caused a rush of worry in Mia's heart. *Do you trust God?* an inner voice asked.

"Come on, sweetheart. I'll get my coat and help you buckle up in Uncle Caleb's car." Mia glanced worriedly from Joel to Caleb. "You won't be long?"

"What I have to say won't take long," he promised grimly. "The car's running, so it should be warm."

Mia looked at Joel. He nodded his encouragement, so with no other choice, she grasped Lily's hand and left.

"You said you'd leave if I asked you to. I'm asking." Caleb kept his voice low so Hilda wouldn't hear. "Leave. Now. Tonight."

"Caleb, it's almost Christmas," Joel protested. "I've got a gift for Lily under the tree. I want to watch her open it. Just a few more days. Please?"

"You can't even keep your word, can you?" Caleb retrieved his coat. "Leave this place tonight. If you don't, I'll make it so you'll wish you'd never come to Buffalo Gap."

To his surprise Joel didn't argue. He simply stood there in his faded corduroy jeans and washed-out shirt, looking dignified yet old. Finally he nodded.

"If that's what you want, I will leave. You'll never hear from me again," Joel promised. "But I'm not running out of here like a thief in the night. I am going to stay until Christmas. I owe that to Hilda and to Mia and to Lily. After that you'll be rid of me."

Caleb was about to argue when Hilda walked into the room. She glanced from him to Joel and frowned.

"Something wrong?" she asked.

"Yes," Caleb snapped, unable to control his fury that his father had won this round. "He is what's wrong. He's a murderer, a liar and a thief. Watch out."

Caleb stormed out of the house, said good-night to Mia, who backed away from his car and studied him with sadness. He climbed into the car, checking to be sure Lily was buckled in the backseat before he shoved the gearshift into Drive.

"What's wrong, Uncle Caleb?" Lily asked.

"Everything." He gunned the engine, then took off around the circular driveway, knowing he was going too fast but unable to stifle his building frustration.

Suddenly Lily said, "A deer!"

Caleb slammed on his brakes, putting the car into a spin on the icy road. He fought to right it and lost as his left front wheel slid off the road and sent the car rolling. Caleb's head slammed into the steering wheel. As everything faded he had only one thought.

Lily!

Chapter Fifteen

❧

"Caleb? Can you hear me?"

The voice was Mia's, tender, oozing love. For him. Could she still love him after what he'd done?

"Lily?" he whispered, every muscle in his body protesting at the effort it took to say the word. But he had to know. Had he hurt her? Had his anger hurt sweet, precious Lily?

"Lily's fine, Caleb. Do you hear me?" Mia touched his cheek, her finger as soft as velvet against his cheek. "Lily is fine. Her seat belt kept her in place. But you have a concussion."

"Lily's okay?" Why couldn't he get his eyes open?

"She's fine. Joel got her out first, then rescued you," Mia explained. "I called 911, but they had to take their time because of the icy roads. Your car rolled and was leaking fuel. Joel thought it might ignite, so he pulled you out to safety."

"Joel?" Though Caleb finally pried his eyes

open and saw Mia with her cape of red-gold hair, smiling at him, he couldn't make sense of what she was saying.

Joel had saved him? After Caleb had threatened him, ordered him to leave?

"I was so scared. You mean everything to me, Caleb. I love you so much." Mia pressed her lips to his, not asking for anything. Just offering comfort. And love. But how could she love him when he was so full of anger and hate?

Everything in his head felt jumbled, disjointed. Caleb opened his eyes again and found peace in Mia. Sweet Mia, holding his hand, loving him.

"The doctors want to talk to you, Caleb. I have to take Lily home. Rest well. I love you." She kissed his cheek, then disappeared. He wanted to go after her, but a hand pressed him down.

"You have a concussion, Caleb. You need to stay still for a while."

Caleb lay awake long into the night as images from the crash replayed in his brain. One cold, hard fact stuck out. Because of his anger at Joel, he hadn't been paying attention to his driving. He could easily have avoided the deer, had done it many times before. But with his mind clouded by anger, he'd nearly killed Lily.

What's the difference between your anger and your father's drinking, Caleb? his brain demanded. *Both led to a loss of control. You are as*

*guilty as your father. It's only by God's grace that
Lily's not badly hurt, or dead, like your mother.*

The truth finally pierced through his anger and
bitterness to shine on the truth. Wrong was wrong.
God didn't forgive by degree. He forgave. Period.
Everyone made mistakes. Some were life changing, like his mother's death, but no less forgiv-
able by God.

At last Caleb understood. His anger wasn't only
toward his father, but also toward himself for not
preventing his mother's death. He'd shifted the
guilt he felt onto his father. He closed his eyes and
let the scene replay. Arguing. His mother stepping
back, falling while his father reached out. Was it
Joel's fault?

Caleb didn't know anymore. All he knew was
that the hate had to be over. He had to ask God's
forgiveness, forgiveness willingly given for him
and for his father.

Sun began to light the eastern sky while Caleb
prayed for forgiveness. Cleansed and restored to
his heavenly father, he finally drifted into sleep,
his thoughts of Mia and the love she had. How
could she still love him now that he'd endangered
Lily?

"Father, You know this child far better than
I do. I love him, but He's Your son, too. Take
away his pain and heal him with Your love. In
Jesus' name."

Caleb lifted his eyelids and studied the father seated next to his bed.

"How can you pray that?"

Joel simply smiled.

"How can you love me after all I've said and done to you?"

"Love is all I have to give you, Caleb," Joel said softly. "I've always loved you, since the day your mom put you in my arms. That will never change. I'll always pray for God's best for you." He rose. "I'm leaving. Goodbye, son."

"Wait!" Caleb struggled to sit up, wincing as his ribs protested. "I don't want you to go."

"I have to. I promised, and I keep my promises." Joel's steady gaze met his. "I'm sorry you can't forgive me."

"I don't have the right to forgive you," Caleb admitted. "It's you who should forgive me." The enormity of his actions replayed through his memory. "I could have killed Lily," he whispered.

"By God's grace you didn't. Lily only remembers the car rolling and hanging upside down. She doesn't have bad memories, except she's concerned about you. And the deer."

"By God's grace." Caleb mulled over the words. He had a father because of God's grace. He had a woman who loved him because of God's grace.

"Can you forgive me, Caleb?" Joel asked.

"I don't know. I've hung on to it for so long that I'm not sure I'll ever be completely free," Caleb answered honestly. He saw Joel's disappointment flare. "But I want to."

"Let's start over." Joel thrust out his hand. "Joel Crane, sinner saved by God's grace."

"Caleb Grant," he said, shaking his father's hand. "Also known as Caleb Crane. Son of Joel and Theresa Crane."

Tears filled his father's eyes as he said, "I'm looking forward to getting to know you, son. It will take time, but with God all things are possible."

"What?" Caleb asked, noting Joel's hesitation.

"Mia loves you, son. I think you love her, too." Joel frowned. "Love is the one thing that can heal you, but for it to do its work, you have to be vulnerable to it. There's no sure thing with love. But to go without it because you're afraid…that's wrong."

"I'm not sure I can love Mia as she ought to be loved," Caleb admitted. "I don't know anything about love."

"Sure you do. You know you'd give your life for her and Lily. You know you want to be with her tomorrow and tomorrow after that."

True, but was that enough for someone as precious as Mia?

"Mia needs you in her life as much as you need her. Lily needs both of you." Joel shrugged. "Why don't you just enjoy that and leave the rest to God?"

Two nurses bustled into the room and ordered Joel out before Caleb could answer, which was all right because he needed time to think things through. And to pray.

He longed to see Mia, to hold her in his arms and hear her say once more that she loved him.

"Mia, will you please put on your dress and fix your hair?" Abby begged with a hint of frustration in her voice.

"But why? What's going on?" Mia knew Abby wouldn't tell her, because she'd already asked a hundred times. Finally she gave in, took the bag with the gorgeous black dress upstairs and changed into it. Abby helped her pin up her hair.

"You look so pretty," Lily told Mia when she returned downstairs. Her small arms hugged Mr. Fudge, the chocolate Lab puppy Mia had given her for Christmas. "Are you going to a party?"

"No." Caleb stepped into the room from the kitchen. "We're going to the ballet. *The Nutcracker*. It's a New Year's Eve tradition."

Mia's breath caught in her throat at the sight of him. He had a vivid navy bruise at the corner of his left eye, which only added to his handsome good looks. She hadn't seen him since Christmas when he'd stopped by to drop off the puppy, then left after sharing Christmas dinner. How she'd missed him.

"Tradition?" she whispered, soaking in his presence as joy filled her soul.

"Isn't it?" he asked, silver eyes aglow.

"Well, I usually go alone." Her gaze locked with his.

"It's probably time to change that part of the tradition, don't you think?" He held out her coat. Mia slipped her arms into it, clamping down on the rush of love.

This was Caleb being nice. It didn't mean anything, she told herself as Lily hugged them and Hilda and Joel promised to care for her.

"Go home, Abby. And thank you." Mia hugged her friend, so glad she'd made the move to Riverbend. That, like much of her life now, was due to Caleb. Dear, sweet Caleb.

She took a moment in the frigid winter night to admire his new vehicle. "A truck? How come?"

"I needed a change." He lifted her so she didn't have to negotiate the high step.

Oddly Mia found it hard to talk to him on the ride into Calgary. She felt shy, as if she barely knew this man who'd suddenly begun having long talks with his estranged father.

Dinner at a posh restaurant was nice, but Mia barely tasted the food, too busy wondering if Caleb was going to tell her he couldn't love her. She sat through the ballet on tenterhooks. Finally on the drive home, she asked, "Why did you do this?"

"You've been acting like a scared rabbit since

we left. I guess this was a mistake." He turned into a lookout that gave them a view of the entire city, its lights sparkling in the night. "I need to tell you something."

Please, God?

"I love you."

She couldn't believe he'd said it or that he meant it. "What did you say?"

"I said I love you. I think I have for a long time. But I needed to be sure." He studied her with his amazing eyes, his words quiet but assured above the purr of the truck motor. "I've searched God for the truth. I've talked to Pastor Don and to my father. I'm pretty sure what I feel is love. For you."

"Oh." Mia broke his stare to study her hands. Dared she believe? Dared she trust?

"Is that all you're going to say?" he asked with a bark of laughter. "I've spent a week agonizing about this and all you say is 'oh'? Mia, come on!" The plea in Caleb's voice was her undoing.

"I love you, too," she whispered.

"Thank You, God." He leaned toward her and pressed his lips to hers, but the console came between them. Caleb grimaced. "Maybe it was a dumb idea to buy this truck," he said, threading his fingers through her hair, which he'd loosened.

"Why did you buy it?" she whispered, leaning in to his touch.

"Because when we get married, you'll need a truck on your ranch. And a bigger horse. I want to go riding with you, and those little ponies you have just don't cut it."

"You really are a cowboy at heart, lawyer Grant," Mia said, and then she didn't say anything for a while as Caleb kissed her. When he finally drew away, she asked the questions that plagued her. "When did you know you loved me?"

"I can't give you the exact day or time," he said. "You grew into my heart and became a part of me. Your grace, your beauty, the way you took on life and made sense of it— I admired you so much. Thanks to God's mercy, admiration turned to love. I love you. I love the way you care for Lily with all your heart. I want to share that with you, to build a home where love joins us. Will you marry me, Mia?"

"I love you, Caleb. I have for ages." She had to ask, "But what about Joel?"

"He's my father." Caleb sighed. "I'll never know exactly what happened and part of me will always miss my mom, but the day I rolled the car, the day I almost killed Lily—" He gulped, squeezed her hand hard. "That's when I realized that I am not qualified to judge anyone, that my anger could have hurt Lily just as his drunkenness hurt my mother."

Mia leaned over to touch his cheek with her lips.

"I haven't got it all down yet," he said quietly.

"I have a ways to go. It will take time to repair the damage of anger and hate and bitterness."

"Love heals," she whispered. She smiled. "I'll help you work through it, Caleb, just as you helped me work through my problems. I'll marry you and help you be a father to Lily. Because I love you." After they'd sealed their love with a satisfying kiss, she leaned back in her seat and asked, "When will we get married?"

"Next year on New Year's Eve?" He lifted an eyebrow. "Isn't it time to start a new tradition?"

"But that's so far away," she mourned.

"I want that time, Mia. I want to court you, to talk over everything with you. I want to get to know my father. I want you to be absolutely certain that your marriage to me is what you want."

"Caleb, you don't have to worry. I know being married to you will be nothing like being married to Harlan," she said, tears in her eyes. "I love you. I never loved him."

"I know." He smiled reassuringly. "In a year, Lily's adoption will be final. We'll have had time to plan every detail of our future."

"Except the parts God will change," she reminded him.

"A wedding, one year from tonight?" he asked.

"A wedding," she agreed, and kissed him with praise in her heart to the Father who asked His children to trust Him, then chose the best gifts for them.

"By the way," Caleb mused as he drove her home, "I never gave you your Christmas gift. I have to tell you the first part."

"Okay." Puzzled, Mia studied his face and saw his smile. "What?"

"Bethany is back at Family Ties with her parents' blessing," Caleb said, a satisfied look tipping up his lips. "She's asked Abby and me to help her find a good family for her baby."

"If that's what she wants, I'm so glad. It's a wonderful gift. Thank you." She leaned over to brush a kiss against his cheek.

"But that's only part of your gift." Caleb pulled a paper from his pocket and handed it to her. "Merry Christmas, Mia."

Confused, she opened it and squinted to read it in the dash light. She blinked, gaped at him, then reread the entire thing once more. "Caleb?"

"You didn't kill Bobby, sweetheart. He died of SIDS, sudden infant death syndrome. Just one more thing Harlan lied about." Caleb touched her face. "Nobody knows why he died, but it was not your fault."

Mia wept all the way home. Then joy moved in as she and Caleb shared their news with Lily, Ms. Hilda and Joel. Riverbend Ranch brimmed with joy. That was exactly as Mia had prayed for.

Epilogue

On December 31 in a candlelight service at Buffalo Gap Community Church, Mia Granger married Caleb Grant. It was supposed to be a small, private ceremony, but who could say no to Mayor Marsha's constituents' desire to see her son tie the knot to the community's most delightful newbie? Unfortunately the event was running late because of the bride's lawyer.

"Harlan bought Riverbend because the mineral rights go with it," Bella told Mia as she held the bride's slim white heels. "That means that all royalties of oil and anything else they find go to you. Harlan commissioned a survey before he died. There is a vein with a precious metal in it. For as long as you live, the money will go to you. After your death, rights revert to the crown. You're a very wealthy woman, Mia."

"In many ways." She hugged Bella. "Thank you for telling me. Caleb and I will talk about it later.

Right now I'm a little preoccupied with getting married. Can you straighten my veil?"

Bella complied, then took her place in a pew beside Mayor Marsha and her husband. The bridal party was small. Lily walked down the aisle first with no sign of a limp, resplendent in a creamy velvet dress with royal blue feathered trim. She held a dainty bouquet of out-of-season lilies that perfectly matched her eyes.

"Okay, Uncle Caleb?" she whispered loudly when she arrived at the front of the church. His thumbs-up made her smile.

The congregation rose when Hilda suddenly changed keys on the organ and began playing a familiar old hymn that had been Caleb's mother's favorite. Mia stepped into the aisle, her arm wrapped in Joel's.

Dressed in a hand-crocheted lace jacket and a long tulip skirt, she walked slowly toward Caleb, her green gaze beneath her long trailing veil concentrated on him. Her magnificent hair was held off her face with a silver band. She carried lilies in a sheaf mixed with cedar greens and tied with a silver band to match Caleb's eyes.

Once Joel had given her hand to Caleb, the couple turned toward Pastor Don to say their vows.

"I will love you forever, Caleb." Mia touched his cheek. "You will always be my beloved husband, a gift from God that I willingly accept. I can't wait to be your wife."

"I don't deserve you, Mia. But I thank God that He's blessed me with your love. You are the part of me that makes every day a blessing." Caleb's next words were for Mia alone. "When I was lost you came and drew me with your love so I could fully experience God's forgiveness. I love you. I always will."

Pastor Don said a few words, then with his blessing Mia and Caleb kissed.

"That's my mom and dad," Lily hollered, grinning from ear to ear as Mr. Fudge came sliding down the aisle. "We're gonna be a family."

The bride and groom embraced Lily, holding her dog, and Joel and Hilda. It was clear to everyone that they already were.

* * * * *

Dear Reader,

Welcome back to Buffalo Gap. I hope you enjoyed Mia and Caleb's story. Isn't forgiveness the hardest gift to give? We get a grievance stuck in our craw, we think the worst of someone or, perhaps hardest of all, we feel deeply wounded by someone else's action. After being so terribly deceived by a man she should have been able to trust, Mia struggled to let herself trust again. Caleb found it almost impossible to let go of a years-long hate for the man he blamed for killing his mother—his own father. If forgiveness is hard for us, don't you think it must be even more so for God? And yet He forgives completely, over and over.

I hope you'll join me for another visit to Buffalo Gap. Until then, I'd love to hear from you via the web at www.loisricher.com, email at loisricher@yahoo.com, on my author page on Facebook or by snail mail at Box 639, Nipawin, Sask. Canada S0E 1E0.

Till we meet again, may you know the depth and breadth and height of God's endless love and forgiveness and may you learn to love Him with all your heart, soul, mind and spirit.

Blessings,

Lois
Richer

REQUEST YOUR FREE BOOKS!
2 FREE WHOLESOME ROMANCE NOVELS IN LARGER PRINT
PLUS 2
FREE
MYSTERY GIFTS

✶✶✶✶✶✶✶✶✶✶✶✶✶✶✶✶✶✶✶✶✶✶✶✶

HEARTWARMING™

✶✶✶✶✶✶✶✶✶✶✶✶✶✶✶✶✶✶✶✶✶✶✶✶

Wholesome, tender romances

YES! Please send me **The Montana Mavericks Collection** in Larger Print. This collection begins with 3 FREE books and 2 FREE gifts (gifts valued at approx. $20.00 retail) in the first shipment, along with the other first 4 books from the collection! If I do not cancel, I will receive 8 monthly shipments until I have the entire 51-book Montana Mavericks collection. I will receive 2 or 3 FREE books in each shipment and I will pay just $4.99 US/ $5.89 CDN for each of the other four books in each shipment, plus $2.99 for shipping and handling per shipment.*If I decide to keep the entire collection, I'll have paid for only 32 books, because 19 books are FREE! I understand that accepting the 3 free books and gifts places me under no obligation to buy anything. I can always return a shipment and cancel at any time. My free books and gifts are mine to keep no matter what I decide.

263 HCN 2404 463 HCN 2404

Name _____ (PLEASE PRINT) _____

Address _____ Apt. # _____

City _____ State/Prov. _____ Zip/Postal Code _____

Signature (if under 18, a parent or guardian must sign)

Mail to the **Reader Service:**
IN U.S.A.: P.O. Box 1867, Buffalo, NY 14240-1867
IN CANADA: P.O. Box 609, Fort Erie, Ontario L2A 5X3

* Terms and prices subject to change without notice. Prices do not include applicable taxes. Sales tax applicable in N.Y. Canadian residents will be charged applicable taxes. This offer is limited to one order per household. All orders subject to approval. Credit or debit balances in a customer's account(s) may be offset by any other outstanding balance owed by or to the customer. Please allow 4 to 6 weeks for delivery. Offer available while quantities last. Offer not available to Quebec residents.

READERSERVICE.COM

Manage your account online!

- Review your order history
- Manage your payments
- Update your address

Enjoy all the features!

- Discover new series available to you, and read excerpts from any series.
- Respond to mailings and special monthly offers.
- Connect with favorite authors at the blog.
- Browse the Bonus Bucks catalog and online-only exculsives.
- Share your feedback.

Visit us at:

ReaderService.com

RS15